# Three Summers

*a Second Chance Romance*

# S. J. SYLVIS

Published: S.J. Sylvis 2018

sjsylvisbooks@gmail.com

Cover Design: Cover It Designs

Editing: Stephanie McFarlin, editS

Formatting: Indie Formatting Services

# PROLOGUE

ONE YEAR AGO

"Stop it, Rowen," I said through my fits of laughter. I hate being tickled, but it's one of those love-to-hate kind of things. I fumble with putting my shirt back over my head because Rowen's taking his fingers and jabbing them into my ribs.

"Seriously, stop! We're gonna ge—," More laughter. "We're gonna get caught; now, stop!" I swat his arm playfully and he jumps back just in time to hit the broomstick; it crashes to the ground with a loud swish and bang, sending a tremor throughout the restaurant. I guess that's what you get when you dip out of work and end up in the supply closet with your boyfriend/co-worker.

We both pause at the sound of the broomstick falling, waiting for someone to come investigate. I stare at his deep brown eyes and he stares back at mine, both of our ears perked. We wait a few more minutes and no one comes. I quickly throw on my red polo and Rowen tucks his shirt back into his pants, then he grabs my hand and pulls me out of the supply closet, quiet as can be. We both peek our heads around the corner, and no one has even noticed that we're missing.

Rowen takes my arms and pulls me to his chest, and I giggle. He whispers, "I love you, and our supply closet adventures." He kisses the top of my hair and adjusts my visor so it's straight on my head.

"I love you more." And I do. I love him with my entire heart. He has it, and he always will. I'm young. I know, trust me, my mom tells me every chance she gets. "Sweetie, you're only seventeen. You're too young to be in love." I stay quiet every time the words leave her mouth. I don't care what she says; Rowen is my true love. When you know, you know.

"Let's go before we get caught." I nod in his direction and I make my way to the back side of the counter. Rowen grabs his yellow bucket full of bleach water and starts mopping the tan tiled floor.

This chicken restaurant isn't the most ideal job I've ever had, but it works for now. I think I'll always be thankful for this job, despite smelling like fried chicken every night and having to wash the layer of grease off my face when I leave, because I get to spend most of my nights with Rowen.

My head whips in the direction of the glass doors as Samantha stumbles inside. She's soaking wet and she brings in a ton of rainwater with her. It's always storming this time of the year. In North Carolina, we normally have good weather for most of the year but when spring hits, it pours and drives me crazy, but I love still this little town more than anything.

"Thanks, Samantha. I just mopped over there," Rowen rolls his eyes at Samantha's soaking wet boots and she laughs.

"Sorrrrrrry!" she grins at him and makes her way over to me. "Got any free chicken for yours truly tonight?" Samantha comes in almost every night that Rowen and I work. She wants free chicken and since it's so late when she comes, I always give her the leftovers.

"You know it. Wipe your feet and go sit down. I'll bring it out." she gives me a wicked smile and wipes her feet rather obnoxiously on the rug under the register, making sure that Rowen is watching her. She skips to the backside of the restaurant and I go sweet-talk our kitchen crew.

"Hey, James, Samantha is here. Can I give her some of your delicious crispy chicken thighs?" I smile sweetly at James and he shakes his head with a little smile playing on his lips.

James is the head cook and he's been here for over fifteen years. They've offered him the manager job so many times, but every time he denies it. He says, "I just like to make chicken. It's in my blood," and turns the offer down. He's an older guy—in his forties. He was born and raised here in this tiny town, and he also tends to his tiny farm. He sells collard greens on the side, and he says, that collard greens and chicken make him happy, so everyone needs to leave him alone. He can appear like a grumpy old man on the outside, but the truth is, he wouldn't hurt a fly. He's especially sweet towards me, and I can't figure out why; he just likes me. I half-think he knows that Rowen and I disappear every so often to the broom closet and he never says anything. Only glares at Rowen and then smiles his wide, white smile at me.

"Here ya go, darlin'." He hands me a batch of chicken and I turn around to take it to Samantha when I hear the ringing of a bell towards the door. It's strange having anyone else come into the restaurant this late at night; it's nearly ten on a weekday. No one comes in this late unless they're desperately wanting chicken at a strange hour, or if they're Samantha. When my eyes make their way to the door, I'm frozen in my spot. My feet feel like they're cemented into the tiled floor.

My gaze meets the two slits cut into the black ski mask

and my heart stops as all the blood is drained from my face. The person is wearing all black. Black shoes, black pants, a black hoodie with the hood pulled up, and a black ski mask. It feels as if time has slowed. I watch as he looks around the room. He spots Samantha who is cowering in the back booths with her hand over her mouth; he spots Rowen who is also frozen in his place with his mouth slightly ajar; then he looks in my direction, quickly glances to James, then Amanda, who is standing with her back to the entrance with no idea that the devil just walked in.

I see the man's beady eyes dart back and forth between me and the register, and then to Rowen. He's deciding what to do first. Everyone is just... stuck. Time has stopped. I hear nothing but my own heartbeat in my eardrums, pounding wildly with every breath I take. He whips out a gun and points it at Rowen and my heart plummets. I drop the bag of chicken as soon as he opens his mouth. "Move and I'll kill you," he snarls towards the love of my life and I have the sudden urge to scream. Rowen's eyes are trained on mine. I shake my head no at him and he continues to stare at me with fear clouding his eyes. I swallow loudly as I avert my eyes to see Samantha; she's hunched in her seat with widening eyes.

The attacker continues to point his gun at Rowen, but makes his way over to me. I'm standing directly behind the counter by the register, with hot chicken splayed at my feet. My breathing is rapid and I'm holding on to the cold metal counter, inching my thumb towards the red panic button placed on the bottom.

"Open the register!" He screams so loudly that spit flies out of his mouth. I find the panic button and my heart flutters with relief. I press it and his eyes widen as he looks down at my hand. "You dumb bitch!" He brings his gun up and belts me in the head with it. I bend down, covering my forehead with my hand as a white pain courses through my vision. The blood rushing down my face is warm and sticky when I reach up and touch it with my shaking fingers. I hear my name briefly leave Rowen's mouth, and then a gunshot. I bring my head up and see the gun pointed in his direction, but it looks as if the bullet has only grazed Rowen. The bullet clatters against the glass window and it cracks, all the way up to the top of the building. I look back at Rowen once more and he is holding his shoulder, crouched on the ground. Before I can even fathom what I'm doing, I leap across the counter and jump on the man's back. My instincts took over the second he shot the gun in Rowen's direction. The man moves wildly, grabbing me by my tiny arms and throwing me beneath his feet, kicking me swiftly in the stomach. I hear nothing but his kicks pounding into my lifeless body. I feel one last hard blow to the head and I'm met with a haze. My vision is blurry, my stomach burning with pain. I feel the blood dripping down my face and onto the floor. I slowly reach up and touch my face, feeling the puffiness of my right eye, and then the bell chimes in the background. I wait. I wait for someone to help me, but no one comes. I look up and I see Samantha cowering above Rowen's body on the ground. He's holding his shoulder and looking up at her shining face, her blonde hair cascading down towards his. My stomach drops when I think he's actually been shot, but I was right before. He was only grazed. His shoulder is bleeding a little but he's staring at her face.

Confusion fills my body and I wonder why she's not making sure I'm okay, too. I'm confused that Rowen is looking up at her like she is an angel sent from God. He hasn't even looked in my direction. I look up at the ceiling tiles and then back to Rowen. His eyes meet mine and they're filled with remorse. My vision goes blurry again and I shake my head in protest, but it feels like my brain is bouncing off a brick wall. I bring my hands to my head and white spots crowd my vision. I pry open my one eye at the sound of James' frantic, southern voice echoing on the phone. He's over to me in seconds, searching my face. He presses his rag on my forehead and soothes me. "It's gonna be okay, sweets. The ambulance is on its way."

"Where's Rowen?" I ask, although my voice comes out weak and in a whisper. Where is Rowen? Why isn't he over here with me, making sure I'm okay? I see James look up in the direction of the back, and he glares. If looks could kill, his would in that very moment.

"It's okay Sadie. I see the ambulance." And I'm met with darkness.

# PART ONE
## SUMMER, 2010

# ONE

"So, how does it feel to be done with your first year of college?" My mom's voice has reached its highest octave as she helps me unload the boxes from my Ford Focus. I have officially ended my first year at Duke. It's been a whirlwind of a year. I've grown a lot in this year, emotionally, that is. I've decreased my therapy sessions from once a month to never. And I've even made some decent friends, Alicia being one of them. Alicia is my roommate, and the first person to actually see *me* since the attack and not as just this 'fragile' girl with a giant scar on her face.

My therapist's voice echoes in my head at the thought of 'giant' scar. "Don't use words like that to describe your scar, or your attack. If you use words like 'big, giant, scary,' you'll always attach those words to that time in your life." To be honest, the scar isn't that bad. I used to think it was terrible and huge and ragged-looking but half the time, people don't even notice it. Or maybe they pretend to not notice. Either way it's not that bad. It's very thin. It follows all the way from the arch of my eyebrow down to my cheek bone.

"It feels like five thousand bricks have been lifted from my shoulders. If I never have to read another Shakespeare play, I'll die a happy girl."

"Oh, come on. Shakespeare isn't that bad!" I smile at the sound of my dad's voice coming from the house. Of course he would back up Shakespeare; he teaches high school English.

"Hi, Dad!" I place my pink shower caddy on the porch and reach up and hug him. His big arms envelope me and make me feel like I'm five years old again.

"Hi Sade, I missed you."

"I missed you too, Dad." My throat constricts like a boa at the hug from my dad, but I distract myself by carrying my shower caddy and boxes inside the house, and I realize that I suddenly feel comforted by calling more than a 15x15 room home for the summer. I loved college and it was good to get away from this town and everyone in it, but I missed home. I missed my parents. I wasn't technically the typical college student. I didn't necessarily want to leave my parents to go off to college to "find" myself, but after the attack and what followed, I was desperate to get away.

"I like your long hair." My dad playfully flips my chestnut colored hair over my shoulder. It's much different than before I left for school. I used to keep it short, to my shoulders, in a spunky type of way, but once I went to college I let it grow. I let it grow because I felt more secure with it. I know, that sounds wacko and it probably is, but somehow my hair feels like security to me now, like it allows me to blend in.

"Thanks. It's kind of annoying, to be honest." My dad chuckles and throws back some peanuts into his mouth.

"I'm gonna run up to my room and get my things settled before dinner, okay?" My mom and dad both nod their heads adoringly and watch me climb the stairs to my old bedroom.

It's strange being back in my house. I didn't come back for Thanksgiving, and then for Christmas, we went on a family vacation to Disney World. I told my mom I didn't want to come back, it was too soon. Honestly, it had nothing to do with the actual attack, but all to do with Rowen. The thought of seeing him over Christmas break made me want to run to the icy mountains of Antarctica. Even the sound of his name made my heart stop dead in its tracks. I couldn't take seeing him. Not then and not now. I'm terrified I'm going to run into him this summer, but there wasn't much I could do to stay away. I had to come back, eventually. Alicia offered for me to stay with her and her mom for the summer, but how would I explain that to my parents? They thought I was over the situation with Rowen, they mainly focused on my attack and my therapy sessions following it. They didn't know that my main concern was this brown-eyed boy. He took preference to everything, which is why I had to stay away... apparently, until now.

When I walk into my bedroom, it's exactly the same as I left it when I went to college. My white and pink flower comforter lays on my bed, untouched. There's stuffed animals on my shelf, followed by an empty picture frame. On my night table, there's a lamp and an old snow globe that my grandparents bought me when they visited the Grand Canyon. My dresser still sits in the same spot, up against the wall near the closet door and my old books are neatly stacked below the oval mirror. I glance in the mirror and my eyes take in my long hair. I decide to pull it up into a high ponytail, not needing the extra comfort of it. Not today, not in my house.

# TWO

Work. My therapist and my parents thought it would be good
for me to get a summer job, and I very eagerly agreed. I
stopped working after what happened last year, and my
parents gave me money to use while at Duke. Not that I really
needed it; basically everything was paid for with my scholar-
ship, but my parents argued to me that they wanted to help
with anything "extra". My phone pings as I shimmy into my
new work uniform, already feeling claustrophobic with its
tightness. I glance down and see a text from Alicia.

**Alicia**: How are things? Have you seen him yet?

    I know exactly who she's talking about.

**Me**: Not yet, and I hope not to. I think I can successfully
avoid him all summer, if need be.

    She texts back within seconds.

**Alicia**: Don't be a hermit just to avoid him. Don't give him that satisfaction. He's probably avoiding u too. G2G, just wanted to check on u real quick.

My shoulders lower as I take in her message. I need to take her advice and be a little more social. It wasn't hard going out with her at Duke because I knew I wouldn't see Rowen or anyone from high school. No one would attach that night with me, so it was safe. But here, it isn't. Everyone knows my business. Everyone knows I was the girl at Finger Lickin' that got pistol-whipped and beat half to death. I was the girl whose boyfriend just left her like the dust after a sports car takes off, spinning wheels and all.

I look in the full-length mirror and scrunch up my nose at my appearance. My mom thought that a summer job at our local country club pool would be a great fit for me. It's a spacious place, not so suffocating like my last job. I know my therapist backs her up on this. They think it's better for me to be out in open atmosphere than to be cooped up in a place similar to the chicken restaurant. It may bring back flashbacks and all that crap, I get it. But at least at Finger Lickin', I was in a sensible uniform. Here, I have to wear a one-piece, red bathing suit that cuts way too high on the hips. I spin around in the mirror and my face scrunches up even smaller when I take in my body. My butt is half hanging out of my suit. Who approved these uniforms? I grab the long work t-shirt and throw it on over my suit. Maybe I can get away with wearing this all day instead of my actual bathing suit; at least it comes down to my mid-thigh.

As I make my way downstairs, I see my mom and dad sitting in our open kitchen. I love the way our house is set up. You walk down the steps, and everything is so open. Wide open. The kitchen is to the right, and it's huge. A big island sits in the middle and a wooden table sits along the windows in the dining room. Then to the left of the steps is our immense living room. It's technically down on another level, as you have to take two steps to be greeted by the carpet, but it's still to the point that you can see into the kitchen.

I meet both of my parents' faces as I descend further down the stairs, and the concern that is etched on them makes my stomach dip.

"Are you ready for your first day?" my mom asks from atop her steaming coffee mug.

"I guess," I say as I shrug my shoulders. I can sense that they're worried. It's almost as if I can smell it on them. I'm only worried that I'll get stared at by everyone at the pool. I'm sure they'll be whispering about what happened last year, a little kid will probably stare at my flawed face, and I'll be reminded that I'm the girl that got robbed, all over again.

"If you're having second thoughts, you can tell us... you know," my dad peeks up from staring at my mom.

"I'm not having second thoughts. I'll be fine, stop worrying." I raise my eyebrows in their direction and grab my keys off the hook. The pool opens in approximately one hour, and I have to be there early to go over protocols and a little training. I already have my lifeguarding certificate, so I have no idea what other protocol we have to go over.

I give my parents both a kiss on the cheek and make my way outside. As I'm backing out of our driveway, I glance back at the massive dining room windows and my parents are standing there, holding hands, watching me in reverse. They really are the best parents in the world. Caring, comforting, never too smothering. I hate to think about what they went through when James made the call to them a year ago, on that dreadful rainy night.

When I woke up in the hospital, I was greeted by bright

lights and beeping sounds. I was totally out of it, trying to pull out my IV a few times before my mom explained what happened. It all came back in flashes, but eventually I remembered everything. I was in the hospital for a week, and every single day, my mom laid beside me. She only left to take showers and grab food and then she was right there beside me with tired eyes. She made sure my pain was managed, that I was getting the best care possible and that I was emotionally okay. I wasn't. I wasn't okay. I had nightmares for months afterwards, and I would wake up screaming for Rowen... only for him to never be there. It was like I was falling into a bottomless abyss each time I woke up, remembering that he would *never* be there. He never came to visit me. The last time I came face-to-face with him was the night of the attack. The night he looked over at me, lying on the tiled floor in Finger Lickin', with a remorseful glisten in his eyes. That was the last time our eyes met. For all I knew, he could still be at UNC.

UNC, that's where he went to college. Or well, that was his plan before we stopped talking. I was going to Duke and he was going to UNC. We both got scholarships that we couldn't turn down, so once we made our decisions we promised each other that we would do long-distance. We'd make it work. I remember the night perfectly, to a T. Both of us, sitting on my concrete porch steps. He had my hand in his lap and he was looking up at the glistening sky. The glimmer of the stars was our only light.

"We'll make it work, Sadie. Because you... " He took my hand and put it up to his warm lips, "You're it for me. You are the love of my life." I stared at his profile and fell even more in love. He was a beautiful human. Guys think it's weird when they're called beautiful, but Rowen, he was. Brown, golden hair. Perfectly sculpted face. He had one of those sly grins that made girls go weak in the knees. His eyes were a deep brown, with gold specks throughout. He was perfect, and he was mine. Until he left. He left, and he wasn't mine anymore.

When I park my car in front of the vastly tall Country Club pool building, I take a deep breath. I'm a little nervous. I'm a little nervous because the last time I actually worked, I was assaulted. I was traumatized, and everything in my life changed. I'm not afraid I'll get attacked again, but I am fearful I'll have flashbacks, and those are almost worse than the actual attack itself.

As I climb out of the car, I'm met with the blistering sun. North Carolina is known for its beautiful weather, but the summers, they're hot. I look to my left and I see the brightest green grass and a few older men. The club is basically full of a bunch of older men, who live for golf and who lavish themselves in expensive lunches with tiny portions. They hold functions here, weddings... and honestly, it's just full of wealthy families who come to swim and judge others. My parents aren't members. We definitely aren't poor, but we aren't rich enough or snobby enough to have a country club membership. I'm guessing they range more than a few thousand a year.

When I reach the door to the country club, I notice the trembling of my hand. I roll my eyes at my anxiety, knowing that this is an aftershock of the attack. I shake my head and straighten my shoulders as I turn the knob, only to be stunned when I find that it's locked. I look around and I see no one. Maybe I'm not at the right place? As confusion sets in, another car pulls up and a tall, lanky guy climbs out. He has aviators on his face and he's wearing a t-shirt that matches mine, although his is much more taut around his arms and chest, and it doesn't come down to his thighs. He has on red board shirts and he's swinging his lanyard around as he walks up to me.

"Hey, you Sadie?" he asks, removing his aviators. He's cute, but I haven't even given another guy a second thought since Rowen. *Maybe that's my problem.*

"Yeah," I say, but it comes out as a whisper.

"I'm Sash, your boss." He shakes my hand and I wonder how he's my boss because he looks close to my age. Weird having a boss your same age. I was expecting someone much older.

"Am I the only one here?" I ask, confused.

"Mmhm." He unlocks the gate and ushers me inside. Only members have a key to the lock and if you're not a member, you have to pay ten dollars at the front building to come swim. Seems expensive to me.

Sash still doesn't answer me and I put two and two together. "My parents wanted me here early, didn't they?" I knew they were being sketchy this morning. They wanted me here early to get acquainted with my new work space; I guarantee it.

Sash looks over with me and his blue irises hold a little guilt. "Yeah... " I roll my eyes and my face feels hot.

"So, I'm assuming you know about my past work experience." Great, just great. He briefly looks at my scar and then back at my face.

"Yeah, but don't worry. I didn't tell any of the other employees and I won't tell them. Just let me know if you need a break or if something is bothering you, okay?" Sash says all this while I follow him throughout the pool area. He's flicking on lights in the locker rooms and the concession, flipping over lawn chairs and opening umbrellas.

I feel a sense of kindness when he says this. He doesn't

seem bothered by it or like he's afraid I'm going to blow up. He just offers stability, and it's nice.

"Thanks, but I'll be fine. My parents overreact a little." I start to help him open umbrellas and I wipe off a few rain-drops from the glass tabletops. Sash only nods his head at me, and we continue to open the rest of the pool with small talk until the other workers show up.

First comes another girl, named Morgan. She's still in high school but she seems like she has a good head on her shoul-ders. She has long blondish-brown hair and she looks a little nerdy with her black-rimmed glasses. I decide right away that I like her because she doesn't stare at my scar.

Soon after Morgan arrives, another girl comes. Her name is Hallie, and I assume she is in charge of the concessions because she's wearing khaki shorts and a work polo. Both girls are nice enough, but I know we're missing one more lifeguard since there's three lifeguard stands. Unless Sash is one, but from what I've gathered, he's strictly the boss.

I look over at Morgan as she's lathering sunscreen on her legs. "Hey, is there another lifeguard coming?"

"Yeah, but he's probably late. He was always late last year. He's a total hottie, just a bit reserved. Just wait until you see him." She wiggles her eyebrows and saunters away towards her chair. Just as I'm about to do the same, I hear the gate clanking. I turn around and have to place my hands on the lawn chair so I don't fall over onto my face. My heart has gone soaring towards the ground and I'm pretty sure it has stopped beating. I grab my chest with my other hand to make sure I'm still alive, and sure enough, I am.

"Oh. My. God." The words slowly drip out of my mouth and his gaze whips to mine. He stops mid-step and we're both frozen in our spots. The boy I'm looking at is no longer the boy I remember. It seems Rowen has changed, too.

# THREE

I'm stunned, frozen, and unable to speak. I feel as if my heart was torn out of my chest and stomped on repeatedly. It's unnervingly similar to the feeling I had the day I realized Rowen wanted nothing to do with me anymore. A million thoughts go crashing through my mind as I grip onto golden brown eyes. It's like my mind is in a whirlwind and every single emotion that a human can have is suddenly swirling through my body.

I don't know what to do and neither does he. He isn't the boy I remember from a year ago. The last time I saw him, he was holding his grazed shoulder on the bleach-soaked floor of Finger Lickin'. My eyes avert to his shoulder, as if I can see the scar through his shirt. What are the odds that we'd both be working at the same place, again? Is this fate laughing at me? I can almost hear her snickers in the background. Neither of us move for a long time. Well, it feels like an extended amount of time; I know how time plays tricks on you when you're in a state of panic.

Sash's voice breaks me out of my trance and I quickly turn

around and busy myself with my lifeguarding chair, struggling to even out my rapid breathing.

"Row, you've gotta be on time this year. I already promised Becky I would have a talk with you." I feel tears welling in my eyes as I'm climbing to the top of my lifeguarding chair. I won't look his way because if I do, I'm literally terrified I won't be able to pick myself back up off this concrete slab.

"Hello, earth to Rowen?" I hear Sash raise his voice a little and brace myself for the sound of his voice. His voice used to be the most calming sound to my ears. It was always soft but rough at the same time. It was soothing, so soothing.

"My bad." I cringe. His voice sounds just the same, maybe even a little raspier.

I sit on my lifeguarding chair as I wait for people to begin swimming, and try to calm the erratic beating of my heart. I'm on the verge of a panic attack; I can feel my throat slowly closing. I feel as if I'm trapped in this awful state of terror. With the sight of Rowen, his stunned state, the sound of his voice, and all the memories we have together thrashing in my brain, I know it's coming. I just have to remember what my therapist told me, "Let the memories briefly pass through your mind. Acknowledge them, then let them pass by without a second thought. Don't let them crowd you. Focus on your breathing." I follow her ghostly instructions. I focus on my breathing and let them cascade through my mind. Breathe, hold, let out. Breathe, hold, let out.

"Are you okay, Sadie?" I peek down and see Sash standing below my lifeguarding chair. He's squinting his eyes up at me, changing the roundness of them into little slants. He adjusts his hand over his eyes, as if he's blocking out the brightness of the sun. "You look stressed… " He says this quietly.

"I'm fine, thanks." I counter with a sharpness to my voice.

I really do appreciate his kindness but I need be left alone to focus on not having a full-on panic attack on my first day at work. Sash nods his head at me warily and slowly walks away. I beg myself not to look in Rowen's direction because I know it won't do me any good, but I just. Can't. Help. It. It's like he's a magnet and his very presence causes my attraction. I look to my left and Morgan takes a seat on her chair, adjusting her sunglasses. She gives me a tiny wave. I look ahead and there's Rowen, smackdab in the middle on the other side of the pool. Now I really have no choice but to look in his direction. He's literally sitting right in front of me! Like he's freaking taunting me. Breathe, Sadie. Just breathe.

It doesn't take long for the pool to become crowded by families with their rambunctious children, splashing and spraying each other. Moms in giant, overpriced sun hats slather sunscreen on their five hundred kids, floaties get thrown by toddlers, and boys and girls of all ages are told repeatedly to stop running on the wet concrete. It's a good distraction, watching the families swim together and listening to the moms gossip about the last function the club had. I almost forget that Rowen is here... almost.

Morgan has informed me that most of the lifeguards swim in the pool during break, just because it's so hot on those tall lifeguard stands. The sun is blazing, and I finally have to take off my t-shirt. A self-conscious murmur flows throughout my exposed body, having my entire butt out for all to see, but it's not like anyone is really staring at my butt, right? The only guys here are Sash and Rowen and sadly, it's nothing Rowen hasn't seen before. I mentally want to smack myself when I remember how Rowen used to grab my butt anytime I was in a bathing suit. He used to whisper in my ear after giving me a light, playful slap on the butt, "I'm a butt guy, I can't help it." I could feel his grin on my ear as he'd nip it impulsively with his teeth. It used to send shivers throughout my body. He had this strange effect on me.

"So, what do you want to do?" I look over at Morgan and she's staring at me. I just got so lost in my thoughts of Rowen that I didn't hear a word she said.

"What did you say? I'm sorry, I totally zoned out." She laughs and shakes her head.

"I asked if you wanted to swim or go get a snack from the concessions." I scan the pool for Rowen but I don't see him, so I opt for the pool. At least I can't be crowded by his presence in the pool.

The cool water feels refreshing on my warm skin, eliminating all my simmering thoughts of Rowen and the past. I dip in slowly at first. The cold takes my breath away, but it warms up in a few seconds and I'm suddenly dumping my entire head under the water. Morgan and I float carelessly for a few minutes as she fills me in on her senior year; she's surprisingly going to Duke next year, which kind of excites me. Maybe I'll have another friend, other than Alicia.

"So, how were the parties?" I laugh in her direction. Such a freshman thing to ask. Well, a normal freshman. I didn't care much for parties at the beginning. I was a total hermit cowering in my dorm room like it'd protect me from all the evil in the world.

"I went to a few after Christmas break and they're fun. They're not super rowdy unless you head over to the frat houses, but they're fun nonetheless." She beams at my answer and starts rambling on about her roommate and how they've already met on a social media site.

They've planned their room out all the way down to their matching comforters. All while she's talking my ear off, I spot Rowen under the shade standing near Sash. I swallow loudly and I know Morgan hasn't a clue in the world, because she's still jabbering on about school. I take in his appearance and notice all the subtle changes. His hair is no longer shaggy and messy. It's a little longer on the top, and styled to the side. His face looks different, too. He no longer looks like a teenager; he looks like a man. His arms have grown dramatically in size, and I can assert that he's been to the gym by the toned shadows splaying around the edges. I quickly avert my eyes from taking in his changed appearance, blinking rapidly and planting my gaze back on the shimmering blue water. Seeing Rowen doesn't only tug on my heartstrings; it burns my entire soul. He has hurt me in a such a terrible and unforgiving way that I don't even want to give him the satisfaction of a glance. I don't even want to breathe the same air as him. It's going to be one very long summer.

When I get home from work, I sit in my car, staring at the black interior, and go over my actions of the day. I hang my head in defeat, closing my eyes only to be met with the smoldering feeling of my attraction to Rowen. I shake my head and shift my attention out the window, focusing on the red bricks that hold up my house. They look so fresh and unsoiled, and I fleetingly wonder what it would feel like to be refreshed and have a clean slate in front of me. The memories of Rowen, Samantha, and the last year weigh me down like all of those bricks are laying on my chest. If I were made of bricks, they'd all be scratchy, decaying, and full of cracks. I want to feel whole again. I want to erase every memory of Rowen and the attack. I want to erase it all. I never want to remember how he made me feel, and I especially don't want to remember the after effects of that night. I've done so good at accepting what happened, but coming face to face with Rowen again... that is making it really freaking hard to keep my sanity.

"How was work, honey?!" My mom is opening the front door before I even reach the doorknob. I should have known they'd be waiting for me. They've probably been worried sick. I walk in the doorway and glance over in the living room. My dad is sitting on the couch with his white socks perched up on the coffee table, watching SportsCenter.

"It was fine," I mumble.

"Are you okay? You look a little pale. Are you sick?" My mom's warm hands feel my forehead, and I jolt away.

"I'm okay, just have a headache from being in the sun all day." Lie. I do have a headache. It feels like my head is smashed between two truck fenders. It's not from being in the sun all day, though. It's from my minor panic attack. Anytime I'd have a panic attack in the past, I'd get a killer headache afterwards.

"It'll take a while to get used to that sun." My dad glances up from the tv then goes back to watching.

"Well, go get some rest. Maybe take a nap and I'll wake you for dinner." I smile gently at my mom and quietly thank God that it's so easy to pretend I'm fine. If only my parents knew what my day really consisted of.

## FOUR

The last time I saw any of my friends from my hometown was shortly after the attack. No one was allowed to visit me in the hospital because my parents felt that my injuries may scare them, so I kept getting flower arrangements instead. Flower arrangement after flower arrangement. I had so many that my dad had to take them home a few times a week.

When I was able to be in the comfort of my own room, after being discharged from the tiny sterile hospital hell, my room smelled of daffodils and lilies. At the time, I loved the smell of them and the vibrancy of the colors, but now every time I see flowers, I'm only reminded of the pitying way people treated me: as if flowers were going to change the fact that my life was spiraling out of control.

The first few days that I was home, my friends Hannah Marie and Anna came to visit. We weren't as close as we used to be, mainly because I spent all my senior year with Rowen, but we were still considered friends. They were sweet when they came, never letting their gazes linger on my wound for more than a few seconds. They asked about Rowen and didn't push me when I cowered back and didn't gush about him.

Everyone at school knew of the attack, and I'm sure they knew of Rowen and I, too. *What* they knew, I had no idea because at the time, *I* had no idea what was going on between us. He wouldn't answer my phone calls, he never came to visit me. Nothing. I got a flower arrangement from his family that read, "Get well soon!" And that was it.

Graduation had passed by without me. The principal and my parents thought it would be best if I didn't attend, and I didn't mind. I didn't want to go and see Rowen, Samantha, or anyone for that matter. People would stare, my bruises and stitched-up face would bother people, and plus, I wasn't even remotely ready to leave my house yet... let alone go to a graduation with five hundred people staring at me.

The day after graduation, I heard the doorbell ring. I was in my room, wondering if it was Hannah Marie or Anna when I heard a small knock on the door. I didn't get up to answer it, but I slowly sat up in bed when the door crept open. At first, all I saw was a giant white ceramic vase with roses inside. I smiled at the sight, but then I saw who was carrying them.

Samantha's straw-colored hair was pulled up into a tight bun on the top of her head, and her face was glowing. She wore a pretty smile and placed the flowers on my dresser. My heart was beating wildly and I didn't know if I should yell at her, or just give her the silent treatment.

"I didn't see you at graduation, so I thought I'd come by and see you." She stood awkwardly near the flowers, with her hands down by her side. I said nothing in response. It was as if a cat had my tongue. She stood and stared at me for what felt like hours. It was so long that I started to sweat with nerves.

"Can you let me explain?" I looked up at her eyes, and they were welling up. I only nodded my head very stiffly, hoping that she could come up with one hell of an explanation.

"I liked Rowen first. I liked him the moment I saw him working the drive-thru on your first day of work." My face was burning. My hands started to tremble as the words poured out of her mouth.

She paced the room the more she spoke. "I liked him, and he always seemed to flirt with *me* when we were around him. I liked him when you two started dating and I bit my tongue any time you would talk about him. I—I... tried to make my feelings go away, but they never did." Samantha wiped tears from her face with the back of her shaky hand, which only made me want to strangle her. "When I saw him fall down after that guy shot the gun, I was terrified. I thought Rowen had died, Sadie."

I interrupted her, "But he didn't... right? I mean, I wouldn't know because I haven't heard from him." My voice was laced with anger, trembling as I spoke.

Samantha looked away at the harshness of my voice. "Everything happened so fast and I was so wrapped up in if he was alive that I forgot you were just hit in the face. I watched as the guy kicked you repeatedly and I didn't know what to do. I was frozen." She stopped talking and I had to sit on my hands so I wouldn't pull my hair out. Not only did she completely dismiss my question about Rowen being alive, she just kept rambling on about her feelings for him. *She* was terrified?! He wasn't the love of her life; she barely knew Rowen! I was livid, absolutely disgusted with her.

I sat up straighter, feeling the contours of my face form a bitter scowl. "So, you went and made sure *my* boyfriend was okay, before you even glanced in my direction? Are you serious right now? What? Were you two cheating behind my back?! Is that why he won't answer my calls?" My voice was rising and I was praying my mom and dad couldn't hear from downstairs. That's all I needed, more sympathy.

"No! Of course not." Samantha intoned, and I wanted to scream at her. I wanted to scream so loudly that my voice would disappear.

I managed to keep my voice even. "Get out." My eyes met hers, and she took a sharp breath.

"What? You thought I would be typical Sadie and forgive you? It took you three weeks to make sure I was okay, and then you come to my house and to defend yourself? The both of you can go straight to HELL! By the way, I'm NOT okay, Samantha." I could feel the tears pooling at my eyes, and it felt like my heart had been ripped into tiny pieces, all over again. Not only did my boyfriend stop talking to me, but my best friend had apparently replaced my role as his girlfriend. I hated them both. I hated them both in that very moment.

I squeezed my eyes as tight as they could go until I heard my door open and then close. Hate consumed me the moment I knew I was alone. I abruptly swung my legs over the edge of my bed and ran over to the stupid ceramic vase that she'd placed on my dresser, hauling it against my bedroom wall. Pink roses splayed all over my floor, water and tiny pieces of ceramic vase scattering the carpet. I was irreversibly devastated. My mom was in my room within seconds, and I fell to the ground, sobbing uncontrollably. It was the first time I cried since everything happened, and in that moment, I was completely shattered. Just like the vase.

The next months I spent in solitude. I didn't see any of my old friends and I surely didn't say goodbye to them when I left for Duke. Hannah Marie and Anna attempted to come over a few times but gave up when they realized I wasn't up for visitors. They texted and called, and each time, I hit "ignore." Guilt consumed me the second I snapped out of my state of despair: they weren't at fault, but I just couldn't fathom being my typical self anymore. Too much had changed.

I never heard from Samantha again, and the hate lessened as I distanced myself from the situation. Some would assume her to be my enemy, but in order to have an enemy, you have to have hate and I don't have room for hate, not anymore. I think hate is a pointless emotion. The last time I felt hate was the last time I saw her, and I never want to feel that low again. So, I don't hate her. I don't think anything of her. But Hannah Marie and Anna, maybe I could call them this summer—maybe I could apologize for my actions. I need friends, and I don't want to be a hermit anymore. I have grown too much this year to be a hole in the ground.

On the drive to work, I literally pray to God over and over again that Rowen worked the morning shift so I don't have to see him today. This is the first time I'll be working the night shift and I'm eager to see if it's less busy than my morning shift. I always feel like people choose to swim in the beginning half of the day but really, the sun is the hottest around three. I wonder if people know that.

When I pull up into my spot in front of that pretty white building, Morgan pulls up beside me, in her scorching red convertible.

"Hey, girly! Looks like we're working together again. I'm so glad; you actually hold a conversation with me!" I smile in her direction and take in her car, scrutinizing it, wondering if her parents have a membership here.

"Do you know who else is working with us today?" I ask benignly, while walking up to the iron gates.

"Yeah. It's you, me, Andrew, and I think Hallie is in the concessions again." Thank you, thank you, THANK YOU, GOD! The more I walk, the lighter I feel. I now have an undeniable pep in my step knowing that Rowen isn't working with me, today.

Morgan stops in her tracks. "Crap! I'll meet you in there. I forgot my phone in my car." I turn and nod to Morgan and when I turn back around, I'm greeted with something solid. At first, I assume I have run into a wall, which wouldn't be that surprising for me, but then I feel two sturdy and familiar hands brace my arms to steady me. I'm so jolted by the touch that I scramble backwards and whip my arms out of his.

"I'm sorry, I just didn't want you to fall backwards." Rowen is so nonchalant, like the touch didn't even affect him. It probably didn't, not like it affected me.

"Are you okay?" he asks, and I scoff. Is he serious? Am I okay? Where was his concern last year? I turn my body side-ways and squeeze through the open gate and his body, feeling the cool iron scrape along my backside.

"Sadie, wait!" I don't turn at the sound of his voice, no matter how badly I want to. I just keep walking to my stand. When I turn back around, I can see him from the gate staring in my direction with his hands slacked at his side, like he feels defeated. I look away quickly, shaking my head and willing the frog in my throat to go away. I will *not* look back. Rowen could be still be standing there for all I know. I'm so wrapped up in his touch that I look down at my arms, half expecting to see scorch marks, but my arms are their normal color. Every-thing around me seems to be carrying on in its normal rhythm, and here I am. Feeling completely out of sorts.

"Hey, what was that?" I look down and I see Morgan standing below my stand with her eyebrows raised. "Do you know Rowen?"

Do I know Rowen? I literally sneer before I answer her, "No, but I used to... "

# FIVE

The work shift went quickly and I was thankful for how busy we were. Between me having to break up a splashing fight between two little girls and an extremely annoying little boy, and from having to place a little red-haired, freckle-faced kid in pool "time-out" on more than one occasion for jumping into the shallow area, I barely had time to even think about what happened with Rowen. Morgan tried to talk to me about how I knew him a few times, but each time I dodged her questions. She finally got the hint and dropped it with a pout on her face.

I look over to my right and Morgan and Hallie are gathering their bags and heading towards the gate. They both give me a tiny wave as they leave and I wave back. It's just me and Sash. I can hear him counting the register aloud so I quickly grab my stuff and murmur a goodbye in his direction while walking to my car. I pause the second I hear the gate slam behind me. Right beside my car is an old, rusty, brick-red Dodge truck, and sitting on the curb beside it is Rowen, his head hung low. I momentarily think about retreating backwards, but I have nowhere to go as my car is mere feet from me. I could tiptoe and hope he doesn't realize I'm sneaking behind him, but that's just immature. It's time to face this head-on. It's inevitable. I have to face him at some point; we work together, for goodness sake.

I glance between Rowen, who has yet to notice me, and the sun setting just behind the grassy hills above.

I take a gulp of air and drone, "How long have you been sitting here?" My voice comes out shaky, and I bite my bottom lip in protest. Rowen whips his head in my direction and immediately stands up and looks me up and down.

His expression is surprised, then quickly changes to timid. "I've been waiting since your shift started."

I feel my eyebrows shoot up, impressed, but I'm quick to put back the blank expression. He used to read me so well, and I hated it. Hopefully he can't read me now, or else I'm in big trouble.

"I've been sitting here thinking of everything I wanted to say to you, trying to find something to say that would get you to un-hate me, but every single thing I came up with wasn't good enough." He pauses, and I cross my arms over my wet chest.

He inches towards me and I inch backwards, so he stops in his tracks. "There's nothing I can say that will erase what we've been through." I turn my head away from his stance and look at his truck instead. The truck that I used to sit with him in on Old Man Henry's hilltop, overlooking the town. The truck that I spent many nights in, him holding my hand, caressing my thumb. The truck that I spent so many nights in, with him on top of me. My heart twinges at the images flowing through my mind and I can feel the burn filling my eyes.

"What we've been through? Don't you mean, what *I've* been through?" He looks at me with confusion.

I shrug. "I mean, yeah, we were both at work on that rainy night, so I guess in that aspect we were in something together, but then afterwards... nope. I was in that by myself." Pain flashes on his face and for a second, I'm glad.

"You're right."

I quip, "I know."

For a while, neither of us says a word. I stare at the rusty fender of his truck with my arms crossed. He stands beside his truck, arms down by his side. I don't care if he wants to say sorry. I don't care if he wants to pretend like he cares now. He didn't care when it mattered. It's too late.

"Will you ever stop hating me, Sadie?" I hate how he uses my name. I hate how it makes my insides clench, and I particularly hate how I don't hate him.

"I don't hate you." I finally get the confidence to meet his eyes and I hold them. I hold his stare. It makes me want to crawl into the fetal position and cry, but I hold them.

"Why? How could you not hate me? I hate myself." Instinctively, I feel my expression soften.

"I don't hate you, because I think that hating someone is too much work. It's a useless emotion and it only crowds your heart. I don't hate you, and I don't hate Samantha. I hate what you did to me, but I don't hate you."

I swear I see his eyes glisten as the words leave my mouth. I've only seen Rowen cry once, and it was when his grandpa died.

I descended my porch steps when I heard the rumbling of Rowen's truck around the corner. When he pulled that rust-bucket up the driveway, I felt the corners of my mouth rise. Watching him descend from the door made butterflies fly throughout my stomach, no matter how many times he did it. I ran over to him, only to stop abruptly when I saw his reddened face.

"Rowen?! What's wrong?" I asked when I ran to his side. He crushed me in his embrace and I felt the salty wetness that dripped down my bare shoulder. My mind was a whirlwind.

"It's my grandpa. He... " Rowen's grasp around my waist became tighter as he cleared his throat. "He had a stroke. He didn't make it." I tightened my tiny arms around his body and instantly felt the hurt pouring out of him. Seeing him hurt, hurt me too. It tore my heart open at its seams, it bled for him.

Rowen's voice brings me out of my memory, "The world doesn't deserve someone as good as you, Sadie." I take in what he says, while never losing hold of his gaze. He's probably right. I should hate him. I should hate him with every fiber in my body. I should hate Samantha and I should hate that evil man that turned my life upside down, but I don't want to be filled with hate. I don't want to give them the satisfaction of turning my tender heart into a hateful one.

"Maybe so." I run my fingers through my damp hair and feel the overwhelming need to clarify to him that, just because I don't hate him, doesn't mean that I've forgotten what happened.

"I don't hate you, and I won't hate you. But I will *never*," I emphasize the word "never" and Rowen's eyes dip downward, "Forget what you put me through. I will never forget how you never checked on me, how you started dating my best friend not even weeks after I had been attacked, and I'll never, ever forget how you didn't even have the common courtesy to break up with me." I quickly walked to my car, leaving him looking as hopeless as that day I realized he never loved me. Not like I loved him, at least.

I slammed my car door, never once looking in his direction. I made it only three miles before I had to pull over and let my sobs loose. I sobbed and banged my steering wheel and in that moment, I let a little hate into my heart. Hate for myself for being so weak when it comes to him.

## SIX

I adore my small town in North Carolina in its entirety, and I especially love being home with my family. I've made it a goal to myself to have a decent summer, filled with family and friends—and to do all the stuff I used to do before everything hit the fan. My town is one of those places that has festivals every other month, sometimes every month. This month is the "Kick-Off to Summer Fest." Basically, it's a bunch of random vendors that set up their booths in the middle of downtown, the roads are blocked, and there's an abundance of summer-ish food. It used to be my favorite thing about summer. But last year... I didn't go. I didn't get to go because I was holed up in my room like a turtle in its shell. I was anxious, scared, and a bit depressed. And sadly, I was more fearful of running into Rowen and his family than about the trauma that had led me to this state.

Rowen's parents own a small furniture business and they often set up a booth displaying their craftsmanship. Rowen's mom, Beth, takes old furniture and refinishes it to make it look distressed, as if it belonged back in the 1800s. My parents have bought a few pieces for our downstairs living room and I have to say, Beth is extremely talented and they make a vast amount of money. Their house is full of antique things and almost all of their furniture is distressed or worn in some way. I used to love it; it felt old but new and was comforting in that way that you'd pull out an old photograph and get lost in the contents and its history.

Just as I'm brushing my hair and squeezing the life out of the brush handle, courtesy of that trip down memory lane, my mom peeks into my room. "Are you almost ready, sweetie?" I keep my expression neutral as I stare into the mirror at my long hair cascading past my shoulders. Today, I need that extra bit of security that my heavy hair gives me. I'm not afraid of the crowd. I'm more afraid of having a random panic attack at the first look of someone with a black hoodie on. I haven't had any flashbacks or attacks since the beginning of college, thankfully, but you never know when your mind might want to play tricks on you. Sometimes it likes to sneak up and strike you at the worst of times.

"Yep, let me get my shoes." I patter over to my closet and notice my mom has somehow made it into my room and is now sitting on my bed. I grab my white shoes out of my closet and sit down to start slipping them on. I glance up at her, and she is watching me with a wary expression. I can feel the dread sneak up my spine with every second that ticks by.

"So, Sadie. I heard something yesterday at my book club." And there it is.

"What did you hear?" I continue to busy myself with tying my shoes, so I don't have to meet her stare.

"I heard that Rowen is working at the country club pool." I sling my head down low. I was hoping I could hide this little bit from my parents because I know they'll only make a big deal out of it, and I guess it is kind of a big deal, considering. "Why didn't you tell me?"

I cringe at the hurt in her voice. My mom and I... I wouldn't consider us best friends, but we do have a strong mother-daughter relationship. I didn't really go through a phase where I hated her; I've always loved and admired her.

"I didn't tell you because I didn't want you and Dad to make a big deal out of it."

My mom hadn't pushed me about how Rowen and I broke up a year ago. She never really asked any questions, probably afraid she'd break me all over again. She heard bits and pieces from Samantha and I's fight, but that was all she really got. Heck, *I* still didn't know why he broke up with me, if one can ever call it a breakup.

"Are you okay with working with him? I can try to find you a new job somewhere else, away from him." Her voice holds a tension that I've never really heard from her before. And, to be honest, her words aren't the first thing that have made me consider finding a new job. But, that would be me running from my problems and I don't want to run away from my problems. "That's unhealthy," per my therapist's words.

"I'm fine with working with him. We don't really have time to talk. Lifeguarding is kind of full of solidarity." She nods her head, suspiciously, as I stand up and adjust my jean shorts. "Really, Mom. I'm fine. It's been a year. I'm over it." Lie, lie, lie.

"Well, you know I'm here if you ever want to talk about him. Or anything. Okay?" She stands up and pulls me into a hug. It's warm and comforting, and for a second, I just let myself fall into her softness.

"I know, Mom. Thanks." I smile up at her and we make our way out of the bedroom and down the stairs, heading towards my favorite part of summer.

◈

THE FESTIVAL IS full of familiar faces. Mainly just the families that I remember seeing in the football stands on Friday nights and at random school activities. Little kids are running around with their ice cream cones melting on the black pavement, and there's about a million different booths set up, all ranging in color. You have the bright yellow stand promoting its homemade lemonade, the white tented booth, displaying homemade jewelry, and so on. I'm sickened that I can't help but glance around the booths, looking for the one that reads "Furniture," but the sick feeling fades when I realize I don't see Rowen's family anywhere.

My gaze shifts to my parents walking ahead of me, side by side, hands clasped together. My mouth twitches upward and my heart grows tender at their touch. I'm lucky. My parents are the most loving parents that I've ever seen. They're affectionate, and the way my dad looks at my mom is full of endearment. They're a team, the two of them. Their relationship and bond is something I aspire to have some day... hopefully, if I can ever close the gaping hole in my chest.

My dad stops walking and turns back to look at me, playfully prodding, "Let's go Sadie." My eyebrows scrunch as I follow his gaze. I laugh, feeling my face relax. He's staring at the inflatable red and blue water slide, smackdab in the middle of the town square. Every summer we'd go down it and race each other while my mom stood below, laughing and judging who won. I always won, and he'd always complain, "It's not fair. You're half my size."

I place my hands on my hips. "But we forgot to wear our bathing suits this year."

After the first couple of years, we finally started wearing our bathing suits under our clothes just in anticipation of the water slide. But I forgot all about it. I forgot, which causes guilt to build within my chest.

"Correction. You forgot yours." I look down and my dad is pulling of his khaki shorts, broadcasting the navy swimming trunks underneath. I can't help my grin and chuckle.

"Come on Sadie! We didn't get to go last year." He pouts a little as he pleads. I look back at the water slide and then back at him. His eyes have a little light lying within and he's beaming just as brightly as the sun on top of our heads.

"Alright, let's go!" I smile, allowing the giddiness to over-take my body.

When we reach the top, I take off my converse and socks and throw them down to my mom, who is standing in her spot. The same spot she always stands in. I peer over at my dad, and he's smiling like a little kid in a candy store.

I ask, "Are you ready?" He nods at me as we take our positions.

I look down toward my mom's brown hair and give her a slight nod. "Okay, guys," she yells.

"One."

"Two."

"Three."

The mere second that the word 'three' leaves her mouth, I'm flying down the slide, gasping as the ice-cold water hits my bare legs. When I land on the soft, wet mat, I realize I'm hysterically laughing. It feels so good to be laughing with my dad on this water slide. It's like the last year didn't even happen. It's like everything is back to normal. We just needed to get over that awkward hump.

My dad stands up and shakes his hair, spraying water all over me, and grimaces. "How did you end up winning, again? I thought for sure I had you because you're wearing jean shorts. Why didn't they slow you down? This is so unfair!" I cackle.

"You can't beat a champion, Dad." We walk off, my dad's

wet arm draped over my shoulder. I feel light, and it's such a distant feeling. Happiness and normality diffuse across my damp body and I never want to let this feeling go.

I watch the water pour down my body while wringing out my tank top and laughing at my dad's complaints of me winning, when I hear a girly rendition of my name. I look over to my left and there stands Hannah Marie. My mouth opens a little as she encricles me in a hug.

"Sadie!" Hannah Marie quickly backs off, as if she is surprised at what she just did.

I smile at her and shyly tuck a few pieces of my hair behind my ear as she tries to rub off the wetness I inflicted on her. "Hi, Hannah. I... I was actually going to call you this week to see if you and Anna wanted to get together." Her eyebrows shoot up in amazement and once again, guilt gnaws at me.

"Of course! We've missed you, Sadie." she says, bubblier than before. "And you seriously look great. College was good to you."

I smile widely at her, taking in her appearance. "You do too." Hannah Marie hasn't changed a bit. She's still sporting her medium-length brown hair with a few subtle blonde highlights. Still the same small body frame, and she still wears the same thick, winged eyeliner.

"How have you been? Good?" she intones, and I'm hyper-aware that she's asking if I'm back to normal again.

"I've been really good, Hannah. I--I wanted to say I'm sorry for disappearing last summer." I don't allow myself to lower my head, although part of me wants to hide.

"Sadie." She grabs my clenched hand. "Don't you dare say sorry. I understand, and so does Anna. Isn't that what friends are for?" I let out a long breath that I wasn't aware I was holding and smile gently at her beaming face.

"Still have the same number?" she asks, returning the smile.

"Yep!"

"Great, I'll talk to Anna and then we will pick a time for all of us to hang out! Sound good?" The gentle voice and smile disappear as her hyper personality resurfaces. At first, before we became friends, I was annoyed by all of her sudden shrieking outbursts in school. She was so obnoxious, but then I just grew to love it.

"Sure, I can't wait." I plaster on a smile and watch her run off towards one of the shopping booths.

I look over at my mom and dad and they're grinning. I know exactly what they're thinking—that I'm back. The real Sadie is back, and she's staying.

# SEVEN

I couldn't help but be relieved that I didn't see Rowen's family at the festival. We'd all have to make small talk and pretend that it wasn't the most painful conversation in the world. Rowen's parents always acted like they liked me, but I wonder what they thought when Rowen and I suddenly stopped spending time together. Were they happy? Confused? Sad? I know my parents were confused and probably a little relieved. They despised how infatuated we were with each other. I would get sideway looks from them when I gushed about him. My dad especially hated our relationship. He was always blasting off about how Rowen would hurt me, and I defended Rowen each time. "You don't know him like I do, Dad. He would never hurt me." And he didn't, not physically, that is. But emotionally... he did more than hurt me. He demolished me. He killed me, and now my dad was right each time he'd foreshadowed how Rowen would hurt me. Now, I feel senseless all those times I blindly defended him.

I decided to stop all the hoping and praying to God on my drives to the club that Rowen wouldn't be there. Instead, I tried a different approach. I started hoping he was there, just so I could get over this undeniable fear of seeing him again. I left him in a vulnerable state the last time we spoke. I say it was a vulnerable state, but I actually highly doubt he felt that way. I was the one who had to pull my car over and calm my sobs before I could head home and pretend everything was fine. Not him.

Sure enough, when I pull up to the parking lot Rowen's truck is parked in the front spot. He's early today, and I remember how Sash told him he had to be there on time from now on. My mind skims over the knowledge that Rowen worked here last summer. Apparently, the attack didn't affect him like it did me. I couldn't leave my house for weeks, in fear that something bad would happen. He's obviously a lot stronger than I am. I wonder if he even had to go to therapy? Probably not. That's just me.

When I walk in to clock-in, Rowen is leaning against the farthest wall, talking to Sash with his arms crossed over his bare chest. I quickly glance away, not even wanting to go there. Even with just a simple glance in his direction, I can tell he is buffer than when we dated a year ago. He's turned into a man, and then I think of my own body when I stared back at myself in the mirror this morning. Have I changed that much? If anything, I feel like I look more kid-like than before. Even with my long hair, I still feel juvenile.

After I hear the click from the clock-in machine, I hang my things in the employee area. Sash says hey and I glance back at him and give him a half-smile. I look over at Rowen and he's staring directly at me. I don't say hi to him, though; I just avert my gaze and walk to my lifeguarding stand where I'll argue with myself for the next five hours for looking in his direction.

In the middle of my shift, still arguing with myself that I've looked in Rowen's direction four times in the last two hours, I make the move to keep my eyes on a little boy who continues to argue with his mom about his floaties. I have to agree, he seems way too old to be wearing the annoyingly bright yellow Mickey Mouse floaties, but I guess if you can't swim, you can't swim. Morgan is directly in front of me on the other side of the pool, sporting her golden aviators, and then Rowen is to my right—which makes it a lot easier to avoid him.

Adjusting my body to shield myself from Rowen and focus more on the ever-busier pool, I watch a hairy dad throw his shrieking kid in deep end, his daughter's little arms and legs doggy-paddling their way back over and that's when I realize, I can't seem to find Mickey Mouse boy. I see his mom, talking on her cellphone and her friend, sunbathing beside her in a hot pink bikini, but I don't see the little brown-haired boy. I look around a little further and I spot the floaties on the side of the pool, but no little boy. My heart beats a little faster, thumping in my chest as I look over at the concessions, hoping he is there... but he isn't. I stand up quickly and stare in the pool. He can touch in the shallow part of the pool by Rowen, but he's not there, either. Where the hell is he? I look down in the deep end and see bubbles. My eyes grow wide, and I can hear Rowen distantly shouting my name and asking what's wrong, but I can't look his way. My eyes stay glued to the bubbling until next thing I know, I'm submerging myself in chlorinated water. I open my eyes underwater, welcoming the burning sensation and I grasp the sight of a blurry figure, frantically waving its arms back and forth. I'm over to him in seconds, not knowing that I could actually swim that fast. I grab ahold of his tiny body and shove us both towards the top.

It takes a few seconds to realize where I am, as I'm sprayed with water from a sputtering little boy. When we reach the side of the pool, I feel two sturdy hands grip my tiny biceps and I know instantly that it's Rowen. When he gets us out of the water, I immediately start slapping the little boy's bare back until his coughs start to die down. For a second, it feels like the world has stopped moving. It's just me and the little boy, our hearts beating fast and our chests rising rapidly. It reminds me of Finger Lickin' a year ago, my throat constricting in protest as flashbacks start to crowd my mind. My slick arms instantly break out in goosebumps as a chill sets forth within my body. I squeeze a little tighter onto the little body in my arms, and then I hear Rowen's voice lulling my sudden state of panic. "Sadie, let go. His mom is here." I shake my head and stare into a pair of large, frightened eyes. I instantly release my grip around the boy and in seconds he is in his mother's arms, sobbing.

The mom's cries are hysterical but between her sobs, she thanks me over and over again, like a broken record. I mumble a response but still still feel in a haze, like I'm in a completely different time and place.

"Whooooa. You literally just saved that kid's life." I look over and meet Hallie's wowed expression.

I feel as if a silence breaks through the crowd, although it doesn't really as Rowen mumbles, "That's what she does, she saves lives... " When I meet his face, I wish I hadn't even looked in his direction. His expression sends a knife right to my gut. We are having a silent conversation, one that no one else knows about. No one knows the meaning behind his words. No one knows but us.

Morgan's voice is booming, "Holy shit, she sure does! We need to give her some type of award or something, right, Sash?!"

"Why don't we give Sadie some time to calm down. Everyone, get back to your stands." I watch as all the feet around me disappear while the murmuring and rowdiness of the crowd still jabbers on.

"Are you okay?" He asks as he helps me to my feet, his judgment bouncing back and forth between the blinking of my eyes.

I shrug, "I'm fine, really. It wasn't that big of a deal."

"Yes, it was. Especially for you." He gives me a knowing look and I suddenly feel very, very small.

Sash puts me in the concession stand for the rest of the night, to give me a "mental break" after I refused to go home. I can't stand being treated like I'm about to shatter at any given moment. I'm fine, and not only does working in the concessions make me feel trapped, it doesn't give me a whole lot of distraction time.

Rowen's voice is on repeat in my head: "That's what she does, she saves people." Is that what I do? Do I purposely risk my life for others? I don't mean to. I just act. I didn't even think about jumping into the pool and what would happen afterwards I just... did. Maybe I have this alternate personality that has a superhero complex. Maybe I want to be the one to save others. Maybe I'm just the self-sacrificing type.

"Are you sure you're okay, Sadie? You can tell me... you know." Sash has been asking me if I'm okay every single hour. He's worse than my parents.

"Boss, I'm fine, for the one hundredth time. I swear; now just relax!" I laugh, as I answer him.

"Okay. Well, then, I'll see you Wednesday, right? That's your next day to work, I think."

"Yeah, I'll be here Wednesday." I force a smile as I start to walk through the gate.

Wednesday is my 19th birthday, and I'm not even bothered that I have to spend it at the pool. It's kind of nice being normal again.

"Sadie." I stop right in my tracks as I hear Rowen's demanding voice. I really wish he'd quit using my name.

I slowly look up and there he is, again. Propped right beside his rusty truck, waiting for me. I hope this isn't a recurring habit, because it's exhausting pretending that his very presence doesn't bother me.

"Are you okay?"

I automatically scoff. "No, no, no." I start shaking my head. "You don't get to act like you care now, no."

I'm totally rolling my eyes in my head, about to bust at the seams. That's not fair! He acts concerned after I save a little boy from drowning, but when I jump a robber to save *his* life, and get beaten half to death... I get radio silence. The dots do not connect.

He whispers, "I've always cared, Sadie." My eyes are as round as saucers. I walk right up to him and slap him in the face, the sound of skin on skin ricocheting through the summer air.

I'm so surprised at my action that my hand automatically covers my mouth.

"Oh my God! I'm sorry! I didn't mean for that to happen." I feel my eyelashes tickle the skin just beneath my eyebrows from my flabbergasted expression.

Rowen doesn't say anything for what seems like hours. He just keeps his head tilted in the direction that I slapped him. I'm afraid to move. Things are becoming even more awkward than before and I didn't even know that was possible.

"Rowen, I'm—"

"Please don't say you're sorry again." My mouth closes, and I'm confused as he turns towards me. His eyes are glossed over so much that I can't even see gold specks inside the brown hue. "You have absolutely nothing to be sorry for. You could slap me five hundred more times, and that still wouldn't even be close to what I deserve." Pain pierces my chest. As much as I hate everything that has happened between us, I still don't want him to hurt. I just can't help it. It's like my heart can't handle to see him in pain.

He blinks for a long time before saying, "I just wanted to make sure you were okay, because I knew that you diving in and saving that boy had to have brought back some awful memories. I know I have no right to care, but I do. I can't help it." I don't respond, because I'm afraid to talk. If I talk, I don't know what will come out.

He takes his hands and rubs them over his scruff in a tired manner and I suddenly feel tired, too, nausea swarming through my midriff. I stand there, taking deep breaths staring at Rowen's white t-shirt, but the only thing going through my head is a replay of the little boy drowning and then a man in a black ski mask.

"Sadie?" Rowen's voice is rough, and then I look up and feel a sudden rush of comfort. I'm fine, it's fine. I'm alive, standing and breathing. I'm fine.

"Yeah… " I whisper. "It did, but I'm fine."

He tilts his head and looks at me. Like, really looks at me.

"I like your hair." He says as a matter-of-factly. What?

"Are you trying to distract me from a state of panic?" I chuckle at his attempt.

"That depends… did it work?"

"A little." He gives me a tiny smile and my heart flutters. I need to get out of here.

"I gotta go." I brush past him, and he stands there and waits a few seconds before coming around the front of his truck to my car window.

"Sadie… " I look up at him and meet the worry forming on his face. His forehead is scrunched, and I see the hollowness under his eyes. "Do you think you'll ever be able to forgive me?" There's almost no hope in his voice and it makes my stomach knot up.

"That depends, Rowen... " I look out the windshield and hear the rumble of my car's engine. "Do you want to be forgiven?"

He doesn't answer, so I put my car in reverse and back out of my parking spot, giving him one last glance. Pain is all I see.

## EIGHT

My parents are beaming with at fact that I'm going to the downtown music festival with Hannah Marie and Anna. I mean, like, they were basically jumping for joy that I was actually hanging out with friends. Real, live friends.

"Have fun, honey! And be careful." My mom gives me a tight squeeze and a kiss on the cheek. I shake my head a little as a grin forms on my face. It's refreshing to be back in my old stomping grounds without feeling like I'm going to shatter at someone's look.

When I step outside, I'm greeted by the simmering sunshine. The humidity in the air has already put a wave in my freshly straightened hair. I decided to think outside the box today and dress a little less homely than I have been this past year. I used to use clothes as a shield, just like with my long hair, but today, I decided that I'm done with that. I'm done with feeling guarded. It may have something to do with the small interactions that Rowen and I have been having. I feel a little less... trapped.

I adjust my black floral maxi skirt so it's straight on my

hips. It has a long slit going up the side, so it actually shows off my legs... ooh la la. I paired it with a white tank top that shows some of my midriff, and I finally dug out my old sunhat from two summers ago. I have to admit, I actually look pretty good. I look like my normal self: the old Sadie. She may be a little rusty, but she's still in here somewhere.

"Holy shit! Look at you! Hot mama!" Anna runs out of the car and throws her bare arms around my neck. "I've missed you so much, Sadie!" I manage a choking laugh as she basically traps all of my air with her death grip.

"I've missed you, too, Anna." I say as she finally lets go of me. I still feel the clawing of guilt from shutting them out of my life working up my back, but I ignore it. I don't want to ruin the day with my depressed feelings.

Anna drags me back to Hannah's jeep. "We have loads to catch up on... " I raise my eyebrows, preparing myself for a ton of gossip.

Chris Stapleton's voice booms from the makeshift wooden stage in the town square, and I can't help but feel at ease. His voice echoes around my tiny body and I find myself actually having a good time. I honestly forgot how much fun Anna and Hannah Marie are. They're hilarious and two peas in a pod, even more so now that they've been to college together for an entire year.

"Want some?" I look over to my right and Hannah is sipping from her sparkling pink flask. I tilt my head to the side and give her a tiny nod. I don't really drink a whole lot, especially because I'm not even twenty-one, but I did drink some at Duke and it was always a nice, blissful feeling.

Before the attack, Rowen, Samantha, and I would always sneak her mom's Seagram wine coolers from the fridge and chug them. We would then, out of extremely poor judgment, jump on her trampoline in her gigantic backyard. It was fun, until that time I jumped so much that I puked in her rose bush. Rowen held my hair back and I was so embarrassed, chanting that I'd never drink again. Expectedly, that didn't last long.

I take a sip from the flask and my throat burns as the liquid flows down it. I basically cough up a lung and realize that it's Vodka, and it's disgusting. I'm more of a Vodka and orange juice type of girl. I don't just sip straight Vodka. I cough and sputter even louder as the liquid burns my stomach.

"Jesus, Hannah. What have you gotten into since college? Die-hard Vodka drinker now?" I gasp through my blurry eyes.

She giggles, "No, but Anna and I definitely had a field day at the frat parties."

Hannah and Anna both go to NC State, which is actually really close to Duke. It's kind of pitiful that we never got together the entire year we were at college. We exchanged texts and said we'd hang out, but we never did. I was too caged up in my own dramatic state.

"So, how was Duke? Did you like it? Meet any hotties?" Anna asks after taking a rather large gulp from the glittery flask, shimmering in the sun.

"Duke was... perfect." A smile overtakes my face, "But, no, my roommate and I both wanted to be single and have fun our freshman year and not be tied down by any guys." They nod in sync.

"So... we heard that you and Rowen are working together." I roll my eyes. But I have to admit, it took them longer than I expected to bring him up.

"Does everyone know?" They look at each other, and then back at me, nodding as they held in a laugh.

I growl, "Of course they do." Situating myself in the grass, I say, "I'm not going to lie; its awkward working with him, but I'm adjusting." And that's the truth. I'll leave out the rest, though.

"We haven't seen Rowen since Kevin's end-of-the-year party last summer, and let me tell you what... " Hannah shakes her head, fixating her gaze on the stage up ahead. "You missed one epic showdown between him and Samantha."

I physically cringe at Samantha's name and the fact that her name was in the same sentence as Rowen's. I say nothing and Hannah carries on with her story.

"I don't know exactly what happened with you and Samantha, but consider yourself lucky that you're not friends anymore."

Not wanting to sound too eager, I calmly ask, "What happened with Rowen and Samantha?" I would probably know if I had a social media account, but I deleted it soon after Rowen and I stopped talking. I didn't want to become obsessed with checking what he was into, and honestly, I didn't want to see those annoyingly happy, magazine-worthy pictures of him and Samantha together. It would take me straight to the freaking grave.

Hannah Marie sat up straight, crossing her legs. "Okay, okay, okay. Well, Samantha was standing in the kitchen, you know the big fancy one in Kevin's pool house?" She didn't wait for me to answer, "Well, she was blasting off about how Rowen left you for her, and they were just taking things slow since the whole... ya know, and they didn't want to rub it in your face." A smile forms on Hannah's lips as she tells Anna to take over.

I whip my head quickly at Anna, anxiously wanting her to get on with the story. "Hannah and I both knew she was full of shit and there had to be more of the story, but we still sat there and listened to her basically describe how shitty of a friend she was, and then... " She pauses, grinning evilly. "Rowen flipped. His. Shit." She looks over at me with her wide, brown eyes and all I can feel is my heart beating so fast I think it's going to fly out of my ribcage.

"He was standing behind her the entire time, and then he yelled at her. Like, really yelled. He said that she was full of shit and that she was, and I quote," Hannah takes her hands and forms pretend quotations with her fingers, "'a shitty fucking friend, and Sadie deserves better.' Seriously, the look on Samantha's face was priceless, Sadie. She was mortified. Her face turned about ten shades of red, and her eyes were so big I thought they were literally going to pop out of her head."

Hannah and Anna start to laugh all over again, but I can't even muster up a fake laugh. I just sit, confused as hell about what I just heard. I threw it in Rowen's face that he and Samantha dated or were still dating, and he didn't correct me. He didn't say anything. Why?

"So, he and Samantha didn't date?" I ask, and I'm irritated that my voice is full of hope.

"Apparently not. We aren't sure of the whole story because we were too afraid to ask Rowen, and then Samantha's family moved shortly after she left for college, so she hasn't been back, not that she would give us any information anyway. She always hated us." She did. She despised Hannah Marie and Anna. She said they were "annoying" and "too girly" for her taste, but really, I think she just hated that I had friends other than just her.

For the next few hours we listen to the music, catch up on all the gossip that doesn't involve me (thankfully), and we make plans for my birthday, too. The night flies by and I don't get home until after ten. I go straight to my room, mumbling an excuse that I'm tired (but really I was hiding the alcohol on my breath, and Hannah Marie was so drunk she had to leave her jeep at the park and walk home). When I finally dive into bed, hoping to fall into a deep slumber, I can't. Thoughts of Rowen and Samantha keep clashing together, leaving me to toss and turn all night.

# NINE

"Wake up, birthday girl!!" I shoot up out of bed to the sound of one of those birthday noisemaker things.

"Oh my GOD!" I take my pillow and throw it over my head, getting away from the obnoxious noise coming from my dad.

"Oh, come on, Sadie. You used to love when I did this."

I peek my head out from my pillow and grimace. "I loved it when I was, like, seven, Dad. Not nineteen." But the truth is, I still kind of love it.

My mom saunters into my room wearing her pink cotton robe with her hair pulled up into a bun. She's holding a piece of cake with a candle in the middle, flame flickering with each step, and my dad joins in on her birthday song. I sit up slowly and smile at the pair of them. I used to hate that I was an only child, but now I think I love it. I don't think I'd be this close with my parents if I had other siblings. I get all the love to myself.

I take a tiny bite of the chocolate goodness, and it melts on my tongue. I stifle a little moan. So, so good and so worth being woken up at the crack of dawn by an obnoxious noisemaker.

"Okay, what are your plans for after work? Anything?" My mom is sitting on my bed, watching me take bites of the cake she made.

"No, I'm going to come straight home, but tomorrow night I'm going to an early 4th of July party with Hannah Marie and Anna." I'm somewhat excited, especially now that I know that Samantha won't be there. She is really the only true reason that I have avoided so many get-togethers involving more people and now that I know she's moved away, I couldn't be happier.

"Well, don't forget this isn't your 21st birthday, little missy." I roll my eyes at my dad's pretend stern voice. He's leaning against the doorframe with a playful scowl on his face. My dad is one of those dads that likes to act all protective and scary but the truth is, he probably wouldn't hurt a fly. He can't help but be friendly to anyone and everyone. Try going to the grocery store with him; it takes twice the normal amount of time because he strikes up a conversation with evvverryone. Even the produce guy.

"I won't, Dad." I climb out of bed and start getting ready for work, bombarded by continued random noisemaker sounds and the awful singing of my dad, popping his head in my room to sing me happy birthday, again.

WHEN I GET TO WORK, I try my hardest to hide and blend in so no one remembers it's my birthday, but Sash ruins that the second he walks into the employee room. He announces that it's my birthday and hands me a gift, allowing my face to turn crimson, matching my lovely bathing suit.

Everyone's eyes are on me and I fight the urge to cover my face. But, no one really lingers on my scar for too long and I don't even recoil. Maybe turning nineteen is like turning over a new leaf.

When I reach inside the bag and pull out the white tissue paper, I feel something hard and cool against my fingers. I bring it out and have to cover my mouth, subduing a laugh.

"Seriously?" I look at Sash and he's holding in his laugh, too.

"What is it?" Hallie exclaims, and I turn the picture around and show everyone. It's a black frame encasing a picture of me on my lifeguarding chair, looking out into the pool. Then right in the center are the words, "Country Club Hero Saves Little Boy From Drowning!" with the date underneath.

"I can't believe you did this." I glance at Sash, who's beaming.

"Oh yes. We are hanging it right here." He already has his nail and hammer out, ready to pound it into the wall beside the clock-in machine.

I laugh and shake my head. "Thanks, Sash." Just as I get the words out, Rowen walks in—late.

"Cutting it close; Only one minute until you're supposed to clock in." Sash's voice booms with authority, but Rowen just rolls his perfect brown eyes.

"What's that?" he asks as he watches Sash hammer into the wall.

"Sadie's birthday present." Sash motions to the picture frame that he has taken from my hands.

Rowen takes in the picture frame, a small smile playing at his lips. I can't get away from him faster if I tried. I dodge any conversation Rowen wants to have by heading directly for my lifeguarding stand. Once I settle on my perch hoping that no one decides to drown today, I tentatively glance in his direction. He looks away quickly, and I'm left to avoid him all day, again.

By the end of my shift, I only managed to make eye contact with Rowen twice. Once while we were switching lifeguarding stands and again in one of my sweeping glances as I checked the area for anything exciting. And I have to admit, a thrill went through my body the second our eyes locked. It's amazing that after everything we've been through, he can still make my body do unspeakable things.

Once again when I reach my car to go home, Rowen is waiting for me, right beside that damn truck. My shoulders slump in defeat. Why can't he just go home before me, for once? That would have been the perfect birthday present.

Not wanting to play this game today, I stand directly in front of him, waiting for whatever in particular it is that he wants to get off his chest tonight. I cross my arms over my chest and stare at his body. His arms are behind his back and he seems... nervous.

"Here... " He pulls his arms in front of him and he's holding a small, white cardboard box. I slowly take it from him and open it up, my throat closing. I'm taken back to one of my favorite memories with him: my seventeenth birthday.

I had a "small" birthday party; basically everyone from my class was invited. My mom ordered pizza and she made a cake. I didn't even get a piece of it because I was too busy making sure that my dad wasn't embarrassing me in front of everyone with his numerous knock-knock jokes. I was a complete basket case because it was the first time Rowen came to my house. My parents knew that we had been dating, but at this point in our relationship we had only gone on a few dates—the movies, football games, things like that. Nothing major.

The party ended well. My dad didn't embarrass me too much, Rowen and I were casual in our affection, and the night was filled with laughter and too much cake. Once everyone left, and I said a brief goodbye to Rowen, my parents eyeing us the entire time, and went straight to my room, exhausted.

It was nearly midnight when my phone vibrated on my night table. I reached over and opened it up. Rowen's name was flashing. When I answered, he was completely out of breath and told me to open up my window, so I did as he asked, flabbergasted. I walked over to my one window, with him still on the phone, and slowly slid my fingers below the wooden windowsill and pushed it up. I looked down and saw nothing until I heard a "psst." Right in front of me was Rowen, sitting in the giant oak tree just outside my window.

I shrieked. "Rowen, what are you doing?"

He gave me that award-winning grin and told me to watch out as he stretched his body as far as it would possibly go, and propped one leg into my window while holding onto the tree with his other hand. In one giant push, he was inside my bedroom at midnight, on my birthday.

"Did you climb that tree?!" I whispered, with wide eyes. He only nodded as he sauntered towards me. He took his hand and wrapped it around my waist. I remember the butterflies flying rapidly in my stomach as his hand touched me. My shirt was so thin that I could feel his entire hand through it. He landed his lips on mine and his hands roamed my body and I felt like I was flying. I remember how when his lips let go of mine, I literally looked down at my feet to make sure they were still on the ground.

"I brought you something," he said when his lips left mine. He stepped back and started to pull his backpack off, reaching inside. He pulled out a tiny white cardboard box and I took it, slowly, with wondering eyes.

When I opened it up, I first saw a tiny note. I pulled it out of the box, and it read, "A cupcake, for my cupcake", and I felt my cheeks rise. Behind the note lay a chocolate cupcake with a little kid's plastic ring on top. I remember laughing and meeting his face. It was such a idyllic moment between the two of us. That memory is so minor considering all that we've been through, but it seems so much bigger now. Especially with him standing here, on my nineteenth birthday, with a chocolate cupcake in hand.

I'm not sure if should be happy, or mad. I can't pinpoint my feelings as I stare at the cupcake. This time, there isn't a note. Just a simple, brown chocolate cupcake. I take a deep breath and the sweetness fills my nose, causing my mouth to water. I look up at him and he is watching me very intently. I shut the lid to the box quickly and continue to stare at him until he finally breaks the tenderness of our moment.

"I thought a lot about what you said to me the other night." My eyebrows dip. "When you asked if I wanted you to forgive me."

My heart climbs as he speaks and I can't take my eyes off his. They have me trapped. I feel completely trapped.

"I do want you to forgive me, Sadie. I do. I really do." I nod my head in understanding until he speaks again. "I don't deserve to be forgiven, but I want you to. So, I promise from this moment on, I am going to do everything I can to make it up to you and I understand if you never forgive me, but I'm going to try until the day that I die." I swallow loudly and I feel like I'm going to pass out. I can hear that tiny voice in the back of my head begging me to ask him the question that's been bugging me since the music festival.

I blurt, "Why didn't you correct me when I accused you of being with Samantha?" He tilts his head in my direction and he looks defeated, again.

"I—" He closes his eyes and then opens them quickly when he starts to speak again. "I thought it would be easier for you to just hate me as much as humanly possible, because I don't deserve to even have a tiny sliver of you." He groans, "I hoped if you thought I did more to you than I even care to admit that it'd be better for the both of us. I'm obviously destructive and you shouldn't be around me."

"Then why are you trying to get me to forgive you?" I question his actions. They don't make sense to me.

"Because I'm selfish. I'm so fucking selfish." He looks pained as the words leave his mouth. Maybe this situation between the two of us has more of an effect on him that I thought. Maybe he hurts just as badly as I do, but... there's still that tiny voice in my head saying, he's the one who did this. He's the one who did this to us.

He gives me one last look and opens the door to his truck. "Happy Birthday, Sadie." Before I can muster up a "thanks," he pulls out of the parking lot, leaving only those tail lights glowing in my view.

WHEN I AGREED to go to this party with Hannah Marie and Anna, I had no idea what I was really getting into. I haven't been to a town party since I was seventeen, and that was way before the attack even happened. I went with Rowen and we ended up leaving as soon as the keg was empty. That's when everyone was getting incoherently drunk; it wasn't our scene. We drove up to Old Man Henry's that night and we spent most of the night in the back of his pick-up, letting the light of moon cascade over our bare bodies. It was a good night, a really good night.

"Do you think this looks okay?" I ask Hannah as I climb into her jeep. I was wearing some high-waisted, ripped demin shorts that Alicia and I found during one of our thrift-shop trips. They were super cute, but I wasn't sure it was my style. I was so used to wearing things that made me feel safe and secure and these... these made me feel the complete opposite. They showed off my long, skinny legs and I swear I could feel a breeze on my butt cheeks.

"Absolutely! Especially with that shirt. You look good." I look down and adjust my tucked-in white tank and make sure my bra isn't showing. I wear my hair down and thankfully the humidity isn't messing with it, yet.

On the drive over to Kyle's, I can't help but feel the nerves jolting through my limbs. It's been awhile since I've seen my friends from high school and a lot of them haven't seen me since I obtained this ragged scar on my face. Granted, it's not that noticeable to me anymore, but to them, it may be.

When we pull through the iron gates and buzz in the number combination that Kyle had given Anna, I take in the huge, castle-like houses. I live in a pretty decent house; it's all brick and it's two stories with more than enough rooms inside, but these houses... they're gigantic. It looks like royalty should live here. Perfectly manicured lawns, bright green grass, not a single blade out of line.

Kyle's house is just the same. He only has one older brother, yet his house could probably house ten other siblings. When we walk through the front doors, it already smells of warm beer and the musk of too many people. There are so many people lingering around that I lose count. Most of them are drinking from aluminum beer cans or red solo cups. Some people are dancing; others are playing drinking games scattered around the living area. In the kitchen, there are three metal kegs, with a line of cups being filled to the brim. The lights are dim and there's a disco ball and a strobe light on opposite corners of the living room. If someone had seizures, they'd definitely want to steer clear of this room. Hannah grabs my hands and pulls me to the back deck, and the second the warm night air fills my nostrils, I feel like I can finally breathe again.

"Jesus, I felt like I was in an alternate reality back there. Kyle went all out for this one." Anna says from behind me.

"Me too. The parties at Duke were nothing like that. They were much more mellow." The parties at Duke were kind of sophisticated, not to sound snobby, but they were. At least the parties I went to. Alicia had been to many parties so maybe she purposely took me to the ones that were mellow. Sounds like something she'd do to shield me.

Right after I'd gotten ready for the party earlier tonight, I'd sent a picture to Alicia giving her proof that I wasn't being a "hermit," as she calls it, and she sent me a text back with nearly one hundred exclamation points, letting me know that she was proud. That had me smiling, but then she followed up that text with another saying I needed to give her "proof" of this "so-called" party. I'd told Anna and Hannah Marie all about Alicia and how she kind of helped me out of my slump after last summer. They had already friended her on their social media accounts.

"Okay, here. Give me your phone and you and Anna go stand with your backs to the back door. This will give Alicia all the proof she needs." Hannah commands, grabbing my phone, and Anna and I trot over to the door. I wrap my arm around Anna's waist and we both stick out our tongues as Hannah snaps the picture.

The flash blinds me for a second, but when my vision returns to semi-normal, I see a scowl on Hannah's perfectly round face. Concern courses through my body. "What's wrong, Hannah?"

"Things are about to get interesting... " Confusion fills Anna's eyes and then I hear her voice.

"Sadie?" My blood runs cold of the sound of my name out of *Samantha's* mouth. I slowly turn around and am greeted with that sandy blonde hair pulled up into a high, teased ponytail. She's wearing next to nothing and she looks a little rough around the edges.

I always thought Samantha was pretty but not exceptionally pretty. She was just normal, and I always felt that her friendly heart made her better than she was on the outside, until her friendly heart disappeared and was replaced by a back-stabbing, semi-crazy friend with a black soul.

"I'm really glad you're here. I... " She walks up to me and she's only standing a few feet away. My face cringes at the smell of her strong perfume. *That's new.* "I wanted to say I'm sorry."

I have to hold back a laugh. "For?" Defensively, I cross my arms. Almost as if I'm shielding myself from her.

"For the thing with Rowen and me. We never met to hurt you. We just, kind of, happened." My eyes almost bug out of my head and I hear Hannah chuckle beside me. Samantha has lost her ever-loving mind.

"Samantha, why are you lying?" I ask, wanting my voice to sound strong, but it comes out full of hurt. I reprimand myself, in my head. I don't want anyone to know that what Samantha has done and apparently is still doing... hurts. It hurts my heart. My feelings are actually hurt. We were best friends, but I guess I didn't know her like I thought I did.

Her face blushes a little as she speaks, "What do you mean?"

Rage. I feel rage, now. Just like that. "Oh, cut the shit, Samantha! Everyone knows that you and Rowen were never a thing." Now Samantha's face is as red as the solo cups surrounding us. I take a small peek around and every single person has stopped dancing, stopped talking, stopped doing everything but staring directly at this drama-filled "chat."

"I... " She is at a loss for words so I help her out a little.

"I don't know why you would try to hurt me so bad. It was enough that I got brutally attacked and that my boyfriend just never reached out to me, ever again. Then my best friend decides to lie about being with my boyfriend?" My voice has completely risen to its highest pitch. My hands are shaking and clenched at my sides. Thankfully, Hannah Marie grabs my clenched fist and draws me back from the ledge that I'm teetering over.

"I think you need to leave, Samantha." My entire body buzzes at the sound of Rowen's voice.

"I can take care of myself, Rowen." I spit out the words and he looks away briefly, taking a deep breath.

"I'm—I," she stutters, and I don't give her a chance to respond.

"There is nothing you can say to redeem yourself, Samantha." My eyes have started welling up a bit, and I instantly curse my body for wanting to cry.

She looks over at Rowen and he scowls at her. She suddenly looks away and I feel so flustered and caught in the middle. This is just one huge mess. It's like I'm the tiny helpless fly stuck in a giant spider web full of lies about to get eaten.

I watch as Samantha backs away and turns slowly when she reaches the back door. I lose sight of her lanky body as she makes her way through the crowd. I'm broken out of my trance when I hear Kyle yell, "HOT DAMN! Welcome back, Sadie!" I quickly look over at him and can't help but laugh. He's wearing nothing but some tiny board shorts and he has an American flag bandana wrapped around his head like a headband. His shaggy brown hair is hanging over the sides in all sorts of different directions. He's pointing the grilling spatula at me. I laugh even harder, and I look over at Hannah and Anna and they're laughing, too.

"It's good to be back." I chuckle, and Hannah Marie and Anna drag me to get a red cup filled with beer. In this moment, I feel more alive than I have since the attack. I scan the crowd and see if I can find Rowen, but I can't. He and Samantha are both gone, and maybe that's how it's supposed to be.

## TEN

The next few weeks of summer fly by. I've been hanging out with Hannah and Anna on my days off, in between spending quality time with my family. My days are filled with laughter and sometimes, I forget about all the bad that happened in the last year. I absentmindedly regret not coming home sooner than the summer. Maybe I would have healed faster if I had just faced the stormy waters. Maybe I would have been happier.

Rowen has kept his distance during work but after every shift, he waits for me by his truck. He walks me to my car, which sometimes includes painfully awkward small talk and sometimes we're just silent. I feel the tension racing between the two of us during work, especially on the nights that the sky has darkened and the air is still. There's so much to say but neither of us want to say anything. I'm not sure it would change anything, and I'm not sure it would help the situation. I'm at a good place, even if being near him makes my heart dance around in my chest.

The one thing I promised myself that I'd do before going back to school in a couple weeks was visit my dear old friend, James. James was one of the few people who came to see me in the hospital. My parents felt that they owed him a big tribute for racing to my side seconds after I was beaten. He kept me calm, and he made me feel safe. He made me feel safe when the entire world was crashing around me. I had focused on his old, wrinkled, soft face until I was met with an abyss of darkness. When he came to visit me in the hospital, his gaze didn't linger on my stitches; he didn't glance at all the blackened bruises; he just simply sat beside my bed and talked about the weather. Basically, anything to avoid what had just happened and I was thankful for it. I'm still like that, which is why it's taken me so long to visit him. But he was a big part of my emotional recovery, and I'd never thanked him. So here I am, driving my little Ford on the narrow blacktop roads smushed between farmland.

When I reach his mailbox at the end of the grassy, makeshift driveway, I laugh. It's a fish. His mailbox is a fish. So strange for someone who doesn't even fish. He farms, and then the rest of his time is spent at Finger Lickin' Chicken. He doesn't even have a lady-friend, which I've always found a little sad. Maybe he isn't into the ladies?

My car's tires pad over the grassy land as I drive the long narrow strip to his house. It's a tiny house. Its color is a bit bland, a mustard-y looking tan hue. The shutters and door are a deep chestnut and the only lively part about his house is the white rocking chairs on the old wooden porch. When I park my car, I peek over at the sky and see the sun slowly creeping its way down behind the treeline, and that's when I see him.

James is a bigger man, so I can spot him easily through the rows of the dark green sprouting vegetables. When I step out of the car and wave him down, I can see his huge glistening white smile reflect abstractly on his dark face. He picks up his pace and I instantly grin at his old worn blue-jean overalls and straw hat.

"Well, if it isn't my Sadie!" he says, as he envelopes me in a huge hug. I don't even mind the fact that he has sweat dripping down his face and that he is completely dirty from head to toe. His hug is comforting, like hugging a sweet black bear.

"I've missed you, James," I say with my face nuzzled in his chest. "How are you?"

He pulls me back and rests his hands on my shoulders. "How am *I*? How are *you*? You look as sweet as ever." I smile at him and follow him to the front porch.

"I hope it's okay that I stopped by. I go back to school soon and I wouldn't be able to forgive myself if I didn't come see you."

"Of course it's okay. I was hopin' you'd come. I saw your 'rents a few weeks ago and they said you were doin' real good. It made me proud." He grins from the side and my heart swells.

"Take a seat. I'm gonna get ya some sweet tea."

Minutes later James comes back out to the porch and gives me a glass of sweet iced tea and when I take a tip, my taste buds dance. "My God, this is good."

"Mmhm, no one makes sweet tea like me. Well, 'cept my mama but she taught me so it's the same thing." I laugh and take another sip.

We talk for a few minutes about school and Finger Lickin' Chicken and all the drama that the workplace has. I ask him about his crops and how things are going on his end he tells me just fine. The conversation is easy and calming until he goes on and asks about Rowen. It's literally like I'm chained to Rowen. When someone sees me, they look for him. When someone sees him, they probably look for me.

"So, how is it workin' with that boy?" My head snaps to

his and I carefully watch him put some chewing tobacco in his mouth and spit the rest of its contents in a tan and brown cup. The smell of the tobacco fills the air and I think now I'll always associate it with him.

"Does everyone in this town know that Rowen and I are working together again?!"

"Oh, now, come on. You know how it is in a small town like ours. Y'all are a hot topic." I roll my eyes.

"It's fine. We're... " What are Rowen and I? Friends? No, definitely not. And we have too much backstory to be called acquaintances. I don't even know what to call us.

"Forgive him yet?"

I scoff and rest my head back on the wooden rocking chair. "No, and I probably never will." Lies.

"Sure ya will." I look over at James and his eyes are wrinkled near the edges. His dark, brown eyes meet mine and he gives me a little smile, basically giving me the go-ahead to spill my heart's contents all over the wooden porch.

"I don't know if I want to forgive him." I whisper and I suddenly feel like pulling my hair down for some extra security. The thought of forgiving Rowen makes my heart feel two things: completely elated and then completely freaking terrified. Once I forgive him, I can't go back. I can't un-forgive him and if I forgive him, I'm afraid of the other feelings that will come to the surface; because no matter how hard I try to act like my heart has called it quits on him, it hasn't. Not really.

"You wanna know what my mama used to say?" he asks, rocking his chair back and forth. I nod my head and look out to the distance. The sun is almost set and it's casting a pretty pink tint out on the horizon. It's stunning, and with all the colors swirled together—it reminds me of love. A beautiful valentine of some sort.

I hear him spit into his cup, "She used to say, 'You can forgive but never forget.'"

I say nothing to James and I just let it sink in. I surely won't ever forget anything that happened that night, or before. No matter how many times I prayed to God and wished that I could somehow erase the memories of Rowen and I, it never worked. I even went so far as to Google witches to see if they were real and could cast some strange, wicked spell on me to forget everything. (FYI- there aren't any. Not in North Carolina, at least.)

"Now, my mom was a lot of things. She was a little crazy, but those words; those are some true spoken words from a lady who had been through hell and back. Take it from her; forgivin' doesn't mean forgetting. It just means you let go." I met his eyes and I suddenly found myself shaking my head. He's right, maybe I do just need to let go.

"A BIG OL STORM IS COMIN', guys!" Sash is jumping with joy as he looks out at the wicked sky. The sun is still peeking through the clouds, but in the distance black and grey clouds swarm; it almost looks as if we are in the movie with the huge tornado that takes down houses.

"Why are you so excited?" I ask, perplexed. He is acting like a five-year-old about to go to the county fair.

"Because... " He swings around and pushes his aviators on his head. "We get out of work if it storms andddd... that means I get to go muddin' later." My eyebrows dip.

"You go mudding?" I exclaim. I can't picture it. Sash is just... not the type that looks like he'd go muddin'. He wears aviators, always has his brown hair slicked back to perfection, his face shaven clean... not the muddin' type I'm used to seeing.

"Uh, yeah. It's fun. You should come with me sometime."

Before I can answer, Rowen coughs and then mumbles, "Are you really asking out your employee. Isn't that, like... against the work employment laws." My face instantly heats up.

"Uh, I'm only her boss for, like, one more week." Sash quips in Rowen's direction.

Morgan interrupts. "Plus, they're only like two years apart, Rowen. It's not that weird." She comes to stand beside me and she has her hands on her hips like she's ready to go to battle, over something so ridiculous... Sash and I mudding. How did we even get to this conversation?

I peek over at Rowen as he incoherently mumbled, "Whatever." I can see his jaw muscles flexing. I half expect steam to come out of his ears by the anger rolling off his body. But, he has no right to be angry. He and I... we're history. Ugly, scary, overwhelmingly sad history.

"Maybe I will go mudding with you. I've never been," I say, giving Rowen a sideways look. Take that, Rowen!

"It's fun! Okay, breaks over. Get back to your stands and whenever we feel the first rain drop we'll kick those annoying kids out." We all laugh and know exactly which group of kids he's talking about.

Unfortunately, I've learned that the club is full of rich families who pawn their kids off to the pool so they can drink at the minibar and go golfing. The kids are spoiled rotten and they act like they're privileged, which annoys me to absolutely no end.

Within minutes of me getting to my stand, it starts to thunder and Morgan blows her whistle. "Pool's closed!" she yells and every single kid gives a groan in protest. We all hurry underneath the canopy area, gathering our stuff when it starts to downpour. This is a wicked one. The parking lot is already looking like a mini pond.

"Alright, I'm making a run for it." Sash says as he pulls down his aviators, I guess to shield his eyes from the rain.

"Me too," perks Hallie and everyone else agrees, except me.

"I'm gonna wait it out. Is that okay?" I say in the direction of Sash.

"Of course, but you know how it is down here. When it rains, it pours."

"Don't I know it," I say, meaning that in every way possible.

"I'm gonna wait it out, too." Rowen says as he strides up beside me. Sash's head jerks back and forth between the two of us and I roll my eyes a little in the direction of Rowen. I guarantee he's only waiting because I am. He wants to stand here and be in this miserable atmosphere, laced with awkwardness, that the two of us set off every time we're near each other.

"Okay, whatever. See you guys tomorrow." Sash says as he darts out into the rain. I watch the rest of my co-workers follow suit, laughing and squealing as the rain pounds on their backs.

For minutes, Rowen and I just stand under the blue canopy, feet apart, not saying a word. Just listening to the rain pound vigorously against the cover. The air is filled with the smell of a good ol' southern rain and chlorine from the pool. I try my hardest to concentrate on the drops and how they fall so carelessly from the sky, but the tension, even in this large area, is suffocating. This is how it's been with us the entire summer, and I'm thankful I have only one more week here. I don't have to endure this anymore once I'm back at Duke.

"I think I'm going to try to run to my car," I say, looking out at the darkened sky. The clouds above us are about to unleash an even harder downpour, which will more than likely accompanied by lightning and booming thunder. The temperature has dropped dramatically in the few minutes we've been standing here and I can't help but associate it with the two of us, out in the open. I feel like I'm about to unleash my own storm onto Rowen; there's just something in the air. It's making me antsy and the more I hold it in, the more I feel like I'm going to explode.

"Yeah, okay. Me, too."

"Ugh!" I yell, and I grab my hair and pull it to the side when I look at him. "You're only waiting because I am!" I stare him down, hoping to make him uncomfortable but his deep brown eyes, just stare back at me. Unmoving, unnerving.

"Yeah, so?" He questions, as a matter-of-fact.

"You're just tormenting me," I utter as I step out into the open area. I instantly feel the coldness on my bare shoulders and a chill sets over my entire body. Just as I'm taking off to my car, I hear the thunderous noise from above. I was right; this storm is unleashing.

"Sadie!!" I hear Rowen's demanding voice right behind me, and I flip around when he grabs my arm. My wet hair smacks against my face.

I look down at his hand and everything around me stills. I feel like the rain drops have frozen in their spots, all around us. It's just he and I, skin touching skin. I swallow loudly before I unleash, "Just tell me why."

He looks perplexed as he takes his hand off me. My arms rapidly break out into goosebumps and I tremble at the crashing thunder above us. I watch him blink the water out of his eyes several times before I speak again. "Why didn't you make sure I was okay? Why didn't you come? You never came!" I yell, through the sob edging its way from my chest. "You never came!"

I watch the rain splatter all around us. Soaking us from head to toe. He stares into my eyes and I blink mine several times as I study his face. His arms go slack and his grey work shirt is completely soaked, giving the illusion that it's black. "I did... " he croaks, and I can see his lips trembling. "But I couldn't face you. I couldn't face the fact that I didn't save you." My shoulders slump and I think I feel my heart shatter beneath my rib-cage. Every single piece of my mangled heart has shattered and fallen to the blacktop. I can almost feel it being washed away with the rain. When I meet his eyes, I can see the tears flowing down right beside the rain drops.

"You came?" I ask.

He backs away slowly, inching closer to his truck. "Yes. No one knew. Your mom was asleep, your dad wasn't there. I came and I stared at you from the bottom of your hospital bed and all I could feel was guilt and shame." He swallows and takes a huge gulp of air through the raindrops. "It nearly killed me seeing you lying there, all bandaged up. You deserved more than me, Sadie." And then he gets into his truck and slams the door shut. I turn around abruptly and get in my car and do the same. We both sit there, in the country club parking lot, in our separate vehicles, soaked from head to toe, cursing the world for being so damn cruel to us.

## ELEVEN

I didn't see Rowen at all since our little episode during the treacherous storm. I had two more shifts and he didn't work either of them. I kept thinking that maybe he went back to school early, maybe he didn't come in on purpose, not able to face me. I feel sick to my stomach that we're leaving things unsettled between the two of us, again. Just like last summer. And strangely enough, it stormed that night, too. I think I'll forever hate storms, now.

My parents are totally bumming on me going back to school, but I promised them I'd come back for Thanksgiving this year. This time around, I'm going to do things differently. I've faced Rowen, even if we seem to be leaving things completely screwed up again, and I've faced Samantha. Both of which were hard tasks, but hey, at least they're done and out of the way.

The thing is, with Rowen, at least, I feel just as bad as I did last summer about what's happening between the two of us. "I couldn't face you after I didn't save you... " What does that even mean? Is he upset that I tried to save him that night? Is he upset that he didn't... what? Somehow blind the guy and attack him without a weapon? The whole situation is messy and confusing and I just wish it could be erased. I used to lay in bed and wonder how things would be if that night didn't happen. Would Rowen and I still be together? Would he still have left me in the end? Was the heartbreak inevitable? I feel like every heartbreak is inevitable. It'll happen eventually, right?

Lost in my thoughts, I hear the doorbell ring. I glance at the clock and it's only two in the afternoon. Dad's at the school for a beginning-of-the-year teacher meeting and my mom is at the grocery getting things for my "back-to-school-dinner." She will take every opportunity the world gives her to throw a little party or plan a fancy dinner. Cinco de Mayo? Yep. President's day? Sure, let's have a presidential dinner on very expensive presidential white house china plates. I wish I was kidding. She should have been a party planner.

"Coming!" I yell, as I'm half-running down our long flight of stairs. I assume it'll be someone soliciting, or whatever. No one ever really comes over to our house unannounced, but I hate it when people randomly do.

As I swing open our red front door, out of breath, I quickly send up a silent prayer to God that my dad isn't home. Because if he were, he'd literally kill the person standing in front of me.

"What are you doing here?! Do you have a death wish?" I cry. Rowen's facial expression is simply... solemn. His posture rigid and tense. Maybe he was expecting my dad.

"I made sure your parents weren't here before I came over. Can I come in for a second?" he asks as I cross my arms. Can he come in? The last time he was in my house, we were in an entirely different situation.

"Uh, I guess. But let's go up to my room in case my dad

comes home early. I wasn't kidding. He will kill you if he sees you." My dad wouldn't hurt a fly, but I'm pretty sure that he values Rowen's life even less than a fly's.

Rowen follows me up to my room in silence. It feels like there's an even deeper tension in the air than there was the other night. Great. When we get into my room, Rowen looks around until he pauses at the window... probably remember how he climbed through it so many times—my 17th birthday being the first time, and a few days before the attack being the last. My heart hurts a little as I think about his lengthy body shimmying out of the window in the wee hours of the night; it seems like ages ago. It seems like that little bit of innocence that we had back then, has long disappeared.

I go over and take a seat on the window ledge, so his eyes can be brought back to me instead of those memories that I know are flashing through his mind. He shakes his head and leans against my pink wall. He looks attractive, with his hair messy on top and a little bit of stubble on his rigid jaw. My heart flutters for a second as I take him in and I suddenly feel butterflies flying around in my stomach.

"I have a proposition for you." I flick an eyebrow up. That was not what I was expecting to come out of his mouth.

"Okay... " I say, scrunitzing him.

"I think you need to take this next school year and think about if you want to forgive me or not." I stare at him for a few painfully long seconds, then I end up nodding my head. Okay, seems fair.

"And if you decide to forgive me, come back to work at the Country Club next summer and I think we... " He looks nervous, as his fingers are twitching a little and he keep adjusting his posture on the wall. "I think we should try to be friends."

My heart catches in my throat. Friends. Friends with

Rowen? My voice comes out weak. "Do you really think we can be friends after... everything?"

He shrugs. "I'm not sure. But I'm willing to try, if you give me a chance," he says in response as he strides up to me. We're inches apart, and I can feel my heart yearning for him with as my mind screams at me to retreat. *Abort mission, abort!*

If my back wasn't to the window, I would have taken a step away from him. His face, his smell, everything about him draws me into him. Erases my hurt. How is it that the one person who hurt me so deeply is more than likely the only person who can take it away? "I'll... " I close my eyes and take a deep breath, bowing my head. "I'll think about it."

He gets down on one knee and meets my eyes from down below. I stare into the endless brown of them and I swear I can feel the love coursing from his body. When our eyes meet, it's like our souls are connecting again, and I hate it. I hate that I'm so affected by him. Just by his eyes.

"That's all I ask, Sadie. I'm just so sorry... " He shakes his head, allowing his messy coffee-colored hair to fall onto his forehead "I'm sorry from the bottom of my soul. I will never stop feeling so ashamed of that night and the past year. Never." He reaches up and tucks a long strand of my hair behind my ear and I can feel my heart beating in them, thumping rapidly from the touch. "I'm sorry." His voice quakes as he stands up and leaves my room quicker than I can even process what just happened. I peek out my window when I hear the door shut and watch him climb into his beat-up, old truck. He bangs his fist against the steering wheel several times before starting the roaring engine, then he drives off down the street. I bring my hand up and place it on my chin, "Well, that just happened... "

# PART TWO
## SUMMER, 2011

# TWELVE

The song "Highway to Hell" by AC/DC is pouring through my car's speakers and I instantly turn the volume up to its highest capacity. The change in my center console is smacking together due to the bass and I stifle a grin as I grab my phone to call Alicia. The second she answers I put it on speaker, so she can hear. In addition to all of our similarities, I found out this year that Alicia is also just as into AC/DC as I am. When she first told me I thought she was kidding and somehow learned of my obsession with the band, but she wasn't. We both just have a love for AC/DC, like two little rock and roll babies. I blame my dad for brainwashing me. AC/DC is his favorite band and he played it for me when I was a baby and then for the rest of my life; so, I kind of fell in love with them by default.

After Alicia and I sing the entire song together, over the phone, I finally turn the volume down and have an actual conversation with her.

"Are you back in the States?" she asks, with more emotion than I've ever heard her use in our entire two years of friendship.

"I just landed a half hour ago; I'm about forty minutes from home. Did you miss me?"

After spring semester ended, I was offered an internship in Haiti by one of my professors to teach children in one of the villages. It was an amazing opportunity, and I snatched it right up. Anything to get me further away from coming back home to deal with the Rowen issue. It was only two weeks, but two weeks was two weeks when you were using time as a buffer. Plus, it was an incredible experience. Seeing the conditions over there, getting to work on my teaching skills, the bright faces of the Haiti children; it was absolutely amazing.

"Duh, only two months and three days until we get to move into our apartment! I was already at the store with my mom buying some decorations. I am so excited." Before I can even interrupt and tell her how I excited I am, too (because seriously, an apartment with my best friend? Who wouldn't be busting at the seams?), she asks a ba-jillion questions about Haiti and if there were any hotties in the internship that stole my attention. There weren't. My last fling was with Mark (I know. How bland of a name is that?). But, it was fun while it lasted... I guess.

Mark. Marky-mark. Ugh. He was in my French class and we were partners for most of the group work that Professeur Mills set up every single week. We were to converse in French, and our final was having to perform a lesson on something in the most romantic language in the world. I, of course, aced it, and Mark and I went out to celebrate—where he kissed me, taking me completely by surprise. But, it was a nice kiss and we all know that I needed a distraction from my last relationship. We were an off and on for the first semester but he became way too clingy, basically stalking me, and plus, I learned that he wasn't my type at all.

Sadly, I also learned that my type revolved entirely

around Rowen. Every single guy I encountered even semi-romantically, I compared to Rowen. *He doesn't make me laugh like Rowen ... He doesn't make me smile like Rowen... His eyes are a shade too dark, nothing like Rowen's...* Blah, Blah, Blah. Alicia actually pointed it out to me. She said, "Stop sabotaging every guy's potential because of Rowen, unless... you still want to be with Rowen." Red flags popped up faster than I could even register the thought, which I, of course, mulled over for months to come. Not only was I mulling over the last thing Rowen said to me before I left for school, but now I had to face the fact that I'm not quite over our little love spurt like I told myself. I was over the attack and what happened afterwards... I think so, at least. The moment Rowen asked me to forgive him and be friends with him, I knew that I would. I knew that I would pretend to think about it over the school year, and maybe I would or wouldn't return back to the country club, but deep down, that taunting voice in the back of my head called me a liar and turned her nose up at my protests. I knew I would return back to the country club, but I definitely need to get over the fact that I had once loved him. I need to let the happy, good parts that we had in our relationship go, because if I don't, this summer is going to end up filled with a whole 'lotta heartbreak.

Not seeing Rowen during all the breaks this year was difficult. In the midst of dealing with Stalker Mark, I was still trying to decipher my feelings for Rowen and was overwhelmed by the want and need to just peek in on him. I have no idea how our paths didn't cross when I was home, and I have no idea how I was able to keep it together at school and not use Alicia's social media to creep on him, but I did. Maybe it was the grace of God.

"LOOK AT THAT TAN!" My mom beams as soon as I park my car in the driveway and climb out. It's not nearly as hot here as it was in Haiti. The classrooms were outside underneath a small shaded area, which really didn't help the heat much. Half the time I was pushed outside of the shade so the children could be covered—they deserved to learn in a shaded area, especially give their housing conditions.

My mom hugs me tightly and she looks exactly same as when I saw her over Christmas break. Still beautiful and vibrant, with her brown hair cut into a bob. As I'm hugging her and soaking in her motherly love, my dad is leaning against the doorway with a smile on his face.

"Hey, Daddy!"

"Tell me all about it!" he says as he whisks me inside the door, grabbing my things from me.

That night, we literally spend all of our time talking about Haiti and my teaching experience there, which he loves to hear about it since he is a teacher, too. I know, it's seems cliché to follow in my dad's footsteps but I really do enjoy teaching. Just like he and my mom said I would. They said I have the "teaching gene," whatever the heck that is.

We laughed all night, especially at my rendition of the song the Haitians sang for us as we departed from the village. My parents 'ooh' and 'awed' at all my pictures that I'd taken on my phone. I already missed Haiti, I probably could have stayed there the entire summer, especially if that meant avoiding Rowen. My throat constricts at the thought of returning to work tomorrow as I toss and turn under my covers. You would think that I would be exhausted from my time in Haiti and traveling back home but nope, I can't seem to shut my brain off. I think I finally fall asleep to a little "Rowen chant" that I made up in a desperate measure to stop obsessing over the next day.

~

IT'S my first day back at the country club, but it's been open for almost three weeks now, which means everyone is probably in the groove and wondering where I am... especially Rowen. I can't help the series of gymnastic flips that occurs in my stomach as I replay all the different scenarios in my head. He probably thinks that I don't forgive him and that I would rather stick a needle in my eye than be his friend, which isn't true, not at all. I thought about contacting him a few times and letting him know I'd be coming back to work and that I'd be late, but I ended up chickening out every time. It shouldn't matter this much... right?

After giving myself a pep-talk about becoming Rowen's friend and no longer an enemy, or worse yet, his girlfriend, I climb out of my car and head into the Country Club with a nervous pit in my stomach. I'm so nervous that I can feel my hands trembling. I'm first greeted by Sash, who all but tackles me in a hug. A little put off at first, I struggle out of his arms and he eyes me cautiously.

"Sorry, we just missed you." My eyebrows crinkle and I laugh a little. I didn't realize I was so beloved here.

"I missed you guys, too. I hope no one drowned while I was in Haiti," I joke back and then freeze in my spot when I hear his smooth voice. My heart picks up its pace and I take in a big gulp of air.

"Haiti? You were in Haiti?" I turn around slowly and take in the beautiful male standing behind me. Rowen's face is tanned and even more sculpted than last summer, which causes me to curse the angels who created him because holy shit, he is beautiful.

"Yeah, I was over there for an internship. No one told you?" He looked right into my eyes and shook his head.

"Oh, yeah. Well, I'm back now for the summer." Things are getting awkward as I stand between Sash, who welcomed me back like the hero that I am, and Rowen, who is looking at me like the little kid in that one movie where he sees all the ghosts.

Sash clasps his hands and smirks at the pair of us, "Okay, well, not to break up this interesting welcome-back charade, but you two need to get to your stands."

I hurriedly go to the lockers and shove my things inside as I pull my long brown locks into a high ponytail. I can feel Rowen's stare but I don't dare answer it. Things are weird, and I'm much more nervous that I thought I'd be. You would think after all the nerve-wracking things that I've been through that I'd be a pro by now, but nope. Nada. Not even a little bit.

"Will you wait for me after your shift?" he asks, raising his eyebrows, eyeing my scar for a brief second.

"Well, I assumed you'd be waiting for me, again. Just like you did last year," I say timidly and cross my arms.

"That's only if you want me to... " He averts his deep brown eyes when he says this, like he's the shy one now. Ah, how the roles have changed.

"I do." I say as I brush past him. I swear, I could hear his held breath release as I walk to my stand, welcoming the shining sun.

## THIRTEEN

My first shift back this summer was a breeze—barely anyone was there. No bratty kids splashing one another, no tiny kids almost drowning... pretty uneventful except for the stolen stares that I got in on Rowen. I never caught his eye, thankfully, because that would be embarrassing, but I got that lingering feeling that someone was watching me; I couldn't help but think it was him.

I didn't recognize any of the workers this year and I'll be glad when I have a shift with Morgan next week. We did meet up a few times over the year, but since she was in a completely different section of campus, it was hard to come by her; plus, she was known for going to all the frat parties. *Surprise, surprise!*

When I gather my things and walk out the familiar, hot, iron gates... Rowen is leaning on my car with his red swimming trunks and white work t-shirt on. I have to give myself a five second pep-talk on my walk over to him. *Friends, be a friend. Nothing more, nothing less. Stop staring at his bulging muscles, stop it!*

"Hey," I whisper. The nerves are eating me up inside.

This is a much different encounter than when we first saw each other, last summer. Then I could hide behind my anger and hurt but now, I have nothing to hide behind. It's just him and I, in the open parking lot.

"So, does this mean you forgive me?" He straightens his posture as if he's preparing for a punch. I stare at his chest for a few seconds before allowing my gaze to level on his but I wish I hadn't. Even if I was going to say I didn't forgive him, this moment, this hold his presence has on me, would completely throw me off... It's... fresh, raw, and energetic, all at the same time.

"I guess it does... " I answer and can't help the small grin playing at my lips.

"I didn't think you were coming back... I—" He stops talking for a beat and fidgets with his whistle hanging low beneath his neck. "I didn't think you wanted to be my friend this summer... but I'm sure as hell glad you're back." He steps towards me like he wants a hug, and I can feel my eyes form into saucers. Touching is out of the question!

I back away as I put my hands up. "Under a few conditions, that is." He stops in his tracks and his expression falls as he tilts his head, raising his right eyebrow. "We are just friends. Nothing more, nothing less. No touching, and no flirting." I narrow my eyes as I say the word "flirting." I literally will not be able to handle it. There are way too many memories involved with him to be acting like that. If he touches me, I'm half afraid my body will permanently marked and it'll mock me and my unsettled feelings for him. It can't happen.

"Okay," he says, softly. I take the hurt in his eyes and pocket it away.

"I feel like this might be a bad idea... " I'm almost surprised at the words flowing out of my mouth; it apparently has a mind of its own today.

"Oh, it's definitely a bad idea." He smiles that panty-dropping smile at me, and I can't help but smile back. "But I like bad ideas." My eyes form into little slits as I'm reminded of the first time we met, when he said those exact same words to me.

We were juniors at Clayton High School and we had just lost our rival football game against Eastwick. The student section was absolutely crazy, jumping, pounding their chests, some people in tears. Samantha and I were just about to leave when Kyle announced that he had a "fantastic idea." Half of my peers were already on their way out of the game, still throwing curse words out to the other team, but Samantha begged me to stay and listen to what Kyle had to say. I thought, at the time, that she had a crush on him but really, she probably only had her eyes set on Rowen.

Kyle announced quietly that he wanted to toilet paper the other team's bus before they headed back home. It was a stupid idea, but Samantha, once again, begged me to help him and the few other guys that were in tune on his plan... one of them being Rowen.

There was five of us: Kyle, Rowen, Jake, Reed, Samantha, and then me. I was no doubt bored with the situation and I just *knew* it wouldn't work, but they all pleaded with me to come anyway.

"Where are we going to get a massive amount of toilet paper in the next ten minutes?" I asked Kyle who was the alpha leader of the pack.

"Just follow me, and be incognito," he said, and I laughed out loud when he started to tiptoe behind the dumpsters leading to the parking lot. There's just something about a tall lanky boy tiptoeing that was hilarious. He looked like a ballerina. When we arrived at his maroon-colored Camry, I looked around, wondering where the toilet paper gods were. That's when he popped the trunk on his car, and that's the moment my jaw hit the floor. Samantha stifled a laugh as he reached in and pulled out an enormous amount of white, fluffy toilet paper. By now, most of the fans had gone home and the tail-lights were dimming as they reached the main road. Kyle passed us all some toilet paper and he quietly led us (once again, tiptoeing) to the other team's bus. I trailed behind the group as Samantha raced up to be in front with Kyle. They were both born to be leaders.

"Not much into toilet papering?" I glanced over at the boy talking to me, and my heart fluttered. It was Rowen, the new kid. We didn't have any classes together and I only briefly saw him during lunch sometimes, but now that I saw him up close, I was at a loss for words. He was attractive and unlike any of the boys I was used to at Clayton High. It was hard to find an interest in any of them, as we had been going to school together since kindergarten. We all had to go through the awkward pre-teen stage together, and let's just say, it wasn't very nice to me.

I shrugged my shoulders as Rowen gave me that grin, the one that still affects me today. "I guess I just don't see the point in it," I said matter-of-factly, and he shook his head as we quietly walked behind everyone else. There were a few seconds of awkward silence until we came up onto the giant yellow school bus parked outside the locker rooms. Kyle briefly gave us the rundown of his plan, which was more or less just him telling us to toss the toilet paper onto the bus and then run away to the bushes so we could see the players' reactions. I scoffed when he counted down from three. Everyone was in their low, hunched state as Rowen and I stood back, both laughing at how serious they all were.

When I looked over at him, he was staring directly at me —then he dipped his eyes down my body and back up to my face. I could feel the heat rise to my cheeks and I quickly turned my head.

"You're kind of cute when you blush," he said, and my heart flipped several times while my eyes widened to the widest they'd ever been.

"I am not," I said, although inside I was swatting away the butterflies swarming around. You know that scene in the wizard movie, where the keys have wings and they're flying around rapidly? That was exactly what my stomach was doing.

"You are."

I didn't say anything as I looked up at him again. He grinned, and just like that, I was swooning. I didn't think I was one of those girls who believed in love at first sight... until that moment.

"You ready?" He nodded towards everyone else throwing their rolls of toilet paper onto the bus. My heart started to beat wildly in my chest; I couldn't decide if it was because of Rowen or the fact that I was doing something completely reckless and out of character.

"I don't know... I think this is a bad idea," I whispered, as I heard yelling from the locker rooms.

"That's okay, I like bad ideas," he said, grabbing my hand and pulling me towards the bus. I smiled at our interlocked hands and began throwing toilet paper all around the bus. As uncoordinated as I am, mine didn't even hit the bus but it was fun, nonetheless. Rowen cracked up at my attempts and then we rushed into the scratchy buses, still holding hands. That was the first time I came into physical contact with Rowen, and it definitely wasn't the last.

## FOURTEEN

You know that moment when your parents look at you with utter disappointment, only to mask their feelings of uncertainty and fear—that's exactly what I walked into when my parents caught wind of Rowen and I becoming friends. I hadn't planned on telling them, but in this small town it's hard to keep a secret like that. I'm pretty sure there is a giant yellow spotlight following Rowen and I around. Maybe even someone hiding in the lush green bushes, writing about our every single encounter... which can't be much, since I have avoided him like the plague. Until now.

It's not that I don't want to be his friend, because I obviously made that very clear by coming back to work at the club this summer but, every time I'm in his proximity, I have to argue with myself over buried feelings; I know they're just feelings left over from our little love stint two years ago, and I'm more infatuated with the old Rowen, the one before the attack and the one that is two years younger. This new Rowen... he's not the same. I have to stop comparing him to the old Rowen. Stop comparing the way he still makes me laugh, and still steals small smiles from me, and I absolutely, most definitely, have to stop thinking about the attack and what happened afterwards. It's like my mind is ready to move past it and become this new rendition of the word "friend," but my heart isn't. It's just still stuck, in the same spot, beating for a boy who no longer exists.

"We're just friends. Just trying to be cordial with each other. We've both moved on, it's fine. Really." I say this to my parents although that tiny voice in the back of my head is shouting "liar" at me, over and over again. I roll my eyes at that stupid, unreasonable voice every chance I get.

They don't look convinced. My dad has his hand perched under his chin with a knowing scowl, and my mom just looks plain concerned. They remember the heartache that I had two years ago, and I get it. I get that they're afraid, but they shouldn't be, because Rowen and I—we're nothing and we won't be anything, especially after I win this marathon battle with my heart.

"I think he has more on his mind than being your friend, Sadie," my dad grumbles as he fiddles with his eggs. I frown and cross my arms like a five-year-old.

"Dad, I'm not the same girl I used to be. If Rowen has other plans than just being friends, which I definitely don't think he does, then he will be disappointed." He nods his head slowly, but his eyes show every single worrisome thought. I huff as I lean back and focus on my breakfast instead of the disastrous idea of Rowen and I becoming friends.

"SO, what do two exes who are now trying to be friends, without touching, of course, do for fun?" Rowen saunters up to me during our last break at work. It's been a week since we've declared friendship and we've only had small talk here and there—talking about college, my new apartment, the internship in Haiti... the easy stuff that comes naturally. When he asks to more or less hang out, I have to get my feelings in order and calm my trembling hands. I don't know why the idea of hanging out with him makes me so damn nervous, except for the fact that my subconscious is giggling in the background, knowing exactly why I'm afraid.

"I'm not really sure. We could go to the festival or something... ya know, surrounded by a lot of people."

He quips, "And a lot of staring." My shoulders slump. He's right. Everyone will be staring, judging, wondering, gossiping... all of the above, but I've learned that if you don't face the scary stuff head on, it'll only weigh you down.

"Sadie? Your phone keeps vibrating, like, every three seconds." I look over at Morgan who is standing in the employee doorway holding my phone.

I get up and slowly walk over to it, hoping that Rowen isn't staring at my exposed butt, because nothing really changed in my body figure in the last year; my butt still hangs out of my bathing suit. We should really work on changing these.

When I look down at my phone, I roll my eyes and grab at my hair. It's Mark. Again. For the five hundredth time since I've landed in the states. It's like he had it set in his schedule when I was coming back; he texted me the moment I landed in Raleigh, and I've ignored just about every single text or call from him. We broke up—if you can even consider it enough of a relationship to require a breakup. It was months ago, but he can't seem to get a hint. Showing up at my dorm room, following me around to my classes, even meeting me at the library when I hadn't asked him to. He. Will. Not. Get. A. Hint.

"Who's Mark?" I jump about three feet forward at the sound of Rowen's voice behind me. That was too close, our bodies were entirely too close. I go to slap his chest playfully but then realize that would mean touching and according to my own agreement, we are not allowed to touch. I slowly bring my hand down and cross my arms.

"Mark and I... dated. I guess. A few months ago, and he can't quite get the hint that I'm not interested anymore, or even was to begin with." I chuckle and feel my face heating up. Why is telling Rowen about this making me feel so... small? It's like I'm two feet tall with a lollipop hanging from my mouth.

His eyes darken when I meet them again. "Dated?"

"Yeah. I guess. We only went on a few dates. We had a French class together, but as soon as I told him I wasn't interested, he wouldn't leave me alone. It's like he's obsessed with me or something." I remember Alicia coming at him with her straighter one night in the dorms... hilarious. As soon as I'm finished rambling, my face suddenly feels extremely hot and I stutter, "I don't mean that he is obsessed with me or that any guy ever would be, but—"

"Why not? I bet every single guy you came into contact with at Duke is obsessed with you, or dreaming of you in some way." His look is scorching and I seal my lips, unable to speak. Do friends compliment each other like this? I don't think so.

Ignoring what he said, I continue, "Anyway, he won't leave me alone. I don't know what to do besides ignore him."

"Why don't you tell him you have a boyfriend? There's nothing quite like that burn to put a stop to it all... "

Before I have time to respond, Sash is telling us to get back to our seats. One more hour and we're off, so I take the time to decide if that's the right thing to do. Telling Mark I have a boyfriend would probably shut him up; he seems like a coward and probably wouldn't want to put himself in danger of pissing off a boyfriend. Maybe I can even embellish my fake boyfriend: "huge arms, very protective, will kill on the spot... " *Bye-bye, Marky-Mark.*

When my shift is over, I check my phone and have three more missed calls from him. It's getting a bit out of hand, so I quickly decide to act on Rowen's plan. Just as I'm typing rapidly on my phone, I hear my name from a faraway distance. I look over at Rowen and by the curious look on his face, he's heard it too. I glance over to the pool area and the only person left is Sash. Everyone else has already dipped out.

"Did you hear someone say my name?" I yell over to Rowen and he nods his head. Then I hear it again, closer this time. My eyes go wide when I recognize the voice and see that stupid Camaro parked just ouside the gate. It's Mark. How the hell did he know I was here?!

"Who is that?" Rowen asks, confused.

I look him right in the eye and say, "How's acting like my boyfriend for a friendly little first hang-out sound?" And he smiles his devious smile right back at me and saunters his long stride toward me, allowing my stomach to deepen its pit.

"Just go along with this, okay?" he says as he wraps his large hand around mine, our fingers interlocked, and I can't even think straight; it's funny that after two years, our hands still fit together so perfectly.

"Who are you?" Mark says, as he glances down at our hands. He looks like such a preppy mama's boy with his blue polo shirt and his neatly pressed khaki shorts paired with some Sperry's. The longer I stare at him, the longer I wonder what the heck I was thinking when I allowed him to take me on a few dates. Anything to get Rowen off my mind.

"I'm Rowen. Sadie's boyfriend. And you are?" Rowen croons this with a little grin to his face. I almost roll my eyes at his cockiness, but then I remember he's basically saving me from a Chester-molester type of guy.

"Sadie's... ." He looks so blindsided, like I haven't been blowing him off for the entire last half of the school year! Get a hint, Mark!!

"Sadie... didn't tell me she had a boyfriend. Is this true, Sadie?" he asks in my direction, and Rowen pulls me closer to his body. I oblige without any fight. Feeling his strong body on my soft one makes me feel like I'm at home.

"Yes. I thought you would have gotten the hint since I ended things with you over *three months ago,* and I've ignored just about every phone call or text." I say as a matter-of-fact, hyper-aware of the nerves swirling inside my stomach.

"Oh... well."

"Leave her alone, or you'll be as black and blue as that stupid car you have." Rowen demands and his voice is full of protectiveness. It feels nice for a moment, until I'm reminded that this is all pretend.

"I... okay," Mark says and I can see him take in Rowen's posture. Mark wouldn't stand a chance against him. He walks away slowly and climbs into his black Camaro SS, with that lame blue pinstripe down the side.

When his tires screech as he leaves the parking lot, I jump out of Rowen's hold and my nerves loosen a little. But not enough that I can meet his face.

"Thanks." I look down at my feet, feeling so flustered.

"It's funny, isn't it... " he intones, and I don't answer. He walks over to me and reaches his hand under my chin and my breath catches at his touch. He tilts my head up and he peers down into my eyes, gracefully. "It's funny how easily that role just came to us... isn't it?" He tilts his head to the side, searching for any emotion that my face might give away. I'm stuck, at loss for words. I suddenly feel my throat close and I can feel the tears wanting to well up inside my eyes. He takes his hand away from my chin and walks leisurely out of the iron gates and to his truck, leaving me to stand there singing, "Friends, friends, friends", inside my head, as if that's really going to help.

## FIFTEEN

Hannah Marie and Anna have taken over my closet searching for something to wear to Kyle's fourth of July bash, the same one he had last year, except it's actually on the Fourth this year. I only have a month left of this summer and I've put a stop to my thoughts of Rowen's and my friendship. We haven't talked since our "pretend" relationship the other day and I'm thankful for it. I have no idea what to say. I feel like I'm treading water in an undertow with nowhere to go. I'm just plain exhausted with our friendship, which is pulling on a lot more heartstrings than I want to admit. Where most college students are wishing their summer never ended, I'm wishing mine never started.

"How about this?" Hannah says as she pops out of my walk-in closet wearing one of my summer dresses. It's pretty, and it brings out the blue in her eyes—only coming down to her mid-thigh thanks to the few inches she has on me.

"Yes! Wear that one, plus it's blue, which is festive for the fourth." I answer, wagging my eyebrows.

"Ooh, you're right! Thanks." I smile, and she throws some random clothes at me. "I found this while searching your clothes and you *have* to wear it." I peel the clothes off myself and give a worried expression. I never thought to pair these two things together, but when I meet her stare I oblige and walk into my closet and get dressed. It's a grey skirt that fits tight around my tiny hips and it hits just above my belly button. Then the shirt she threw at me confuses me. It's just a tight t-shirt, and when I look down at my ensemble, I'm concerned. I look stupid. I walk out of the closet and Anna laughs at me.

"This looks ridiculous," I say, taking in my outfit in the full-length mirror.

"Of course it does; you have to do this... " She pads over to me, with her (my) blue dress swishing, and grabs the bottom hem of my shirt, tying it into a knot just below my bra. Then she grabs my messy ponytail and releases it, allowing my hair to fall down my back. She grabs some fancy hair product from her oversized floral bag and spritzes it into my roots so much that I choke on the fresh coconut smell.

After regaining some even breathing, I turn around in the mirror, prepared for humiliation. But she was right. It looks much better like this and I look semi-hot... something I don't feel very often. The white shirt reflects back on the small tanned portion of my stomach and my hair looks casually wavy, falling down around my shoulders.

"You know, you should be a stylist or something," I say as I look over at her knowing grin. She's good at this, seriously.

After Anna and I are ready, Hannah Marie takes her sweet time, applying makeup like fine art.

I can't help but ask the gnawing question in the back of my mind, "Do y'all think Samantha will be there this year?" I know last year she was here visiting her grandmother, but I can't ease away the sinking feeling that'll she be here tonight. I haven't thought a lot about Samantha over the last year, which

I guess means I am, in fact, over the issues we had in our "friendship." It's easier to be a friend to Rowen, and I'm not sure why. Maybe because I once loved him. Not that I didn't love Samantha, but a friend kind of love is much different than a soul-crushing first love with a boy. First loves are raw and unforgiving, just like the heartbreak that comes afterwards.

"No, she is in Peru or somewhere fancy like that. I saw it on social media." Relief floods my body and I let out a breath I didn't even realize I was holding. Thank God.

When we pull up to the party, it's the exact same as last year—cars ranging from Range Rovers to beat up Toyotas line the driveway and the impeccable green lawn. The house is bigger than most houses in our small town, and tons of people are casually strolling in and out of it. I'm ready for a good night tonight; I'm not the same Sadie I was last year when I was afraid of seeing everyone again. I'm friends with Rowen, Samantha and I have closed the chapter on our friendship (or "fakeship" as Hannah Marie likes to call it), and I'm free from annoying calls from Mark. I didn't realize how bothersome they were, and I really didn't realize just how obsessed he was with me until he showed up at my work, which was quite alarming if I truly think about it.

Hannah, Anna, and I take a three-person selfie so I can send it to Alicia, again. Just like last year. "It's a tradition," Anna says while snapping the picture. Then she types, "We miss you!" before firing it off to Alicia. They finally met Alicia during our second semester; we met up a few times through the school year... another thing that was different from last year.

"Sadie!" I hear Kyle yell my name and he all but tackles me into a hug. "I'm so glad you came. I have something rad to show you." Kyle used to be my good friend, even before

Rowen. We basically grew up together, going to grade school, middle, and then high school together. I've never seen him in a romantic way, but I wonder, if I hadn't seen Rowen my junior year, if I would have fallen for Kyle. He's cute enough; he has that boy-ish vibe to him, even now at age twenty.

"What do you have to show me?" I ask as he takes my hands and guides me through the house. I don't see Rowen yet, and I have to put up a mental block so I don't accidently hope he shows. Friends, we're just friends.

When we reach the elegant wrought-iron bannister gracing the stairs to the next level, leading upstairs, I casually take my hand out of his and follow him up, watching his blonde hair bounce with every step. When we get to the top, there's one long hallway of several rooms. I remember where his room is exactly. I know what you're thinking, and I've only been up here because Kyle used to have his birthday parties here, and we'd all come upstairs playing hide-and-seek. I have never hooked up with Kyle and I won't ever hook up with him; he's too close to Rowen and it would be painful and awkward.

"Here, come look," he says, nodding toward to his room. It's much different in here than when we were kids. His red and blue walls are now painted a deep grey, and there's no longer that pesky toy chest in the corner that I'd hidden in during an epic hide-and-seek game. There's no longer clothes piling the floors; it's tidy and precise, not much like the Kyle I know.

Over the music blaring downstairs, I say, "Redecorate?" and he grins.

"My mom did... you know how she is." I laugh. His mom is the type of woman who likes to indulge herself with expensive things, especially her house décor. I get it; if I had all that money I'd want to spend it on nice things, too.

I sit on Kyle's bed, crossing my legs since I have this skirt on that doesn't do much to hide my legs or crotch, as he walks over to his closet. He pulls out a large piece of paper, like the size of a poster, and I eye him suspiciously until I see what he's holding. I jump up in excitement. It's an ACDC poster, the famous one with the words "Highway to Hell" plastered on the bottom below their bodies. The silver autographs shimmer in the one light beaming from up above.

"Oh my GOD! How did you get this?" I take it from his hands, carefully, running my fingers over the autographs.

"My dad scored it for me at some auction of his. He bid on it and didn't really have anywhere for it, especially with my mom's disapproval, so he gave it to me. I instantly thought of you." I smile up at him and put my attention back on the poster. "I remember how you and Rowen always jammed to it back in the day."

"We all did," I say, my eyes glued to the autographs.

"I want you to have it." My head snaps up so hard I'm half expecting it to just fall off my neck.

"What? No!"

"Yes!" He mocks my high-pitched voice.

"It's too expensive. This is worth a lot of money, Kyle." I don't think I own something worth this much, maybe my car, but I don't even own that. My parents do.

Kyle rolls his eyes, "My family has way too much money. Plus, I know you'll never sell it." I hug the poster to my chest because he's right. I won't sell this; I'll cherish it forever.

"But what will your dad say if he knows it's gone?" I've met Kyle's dad before, and his mother. Heck, I've met his whole family and even though they come from A LOT of money, they're all genuine and nice. He's lucky because I've met some guys at college who come from money, and it seems like that's all they've been taught to care about.

"Then I'll tell him I gave it to the prettiest girl I know." He says matter-of-factly and I blush when I grimace at him.

"What? Are you not used to people telling you you're pretty? Because you are." I shrug my shoulders.

"I've just been so guarded the last couple years that I haven't really paid much attention to when someone says that. For the first year after everything, I hid because I was embarrassed at this... " I point to my scar and his eyes follow the curve of it. They fill with pity and I'm quick to rebut. "Don't feel bad. I'm good now; I don't feel the need to hide it anymore."

He smiles and says, "Good. Because your face is too pretty to hide." He gently pushes my shoulder and we're back to our playful relationship that we've had for years.

"Okay, enough compliments!" I put my hand up. "But thanks for this, it's amazing."

He smiles and he wraps his arm around my shoulders as we start to move down the long, hallway filled with bedrooms. "So, have any boyfriends back at Duke?" First he starts complimenting me, and now he's asking if I'm taken... this seems very unlike Kyle.

"Well... " I start by telling him the brief story of Mark and how Rowen had to act like my boyfriend at the club the other day to shoo him away, leaving out all the unnecessary feelings that were lingering in the air when Rowen and I touched, of course.

"So, what's the deal with you two?"

Playing dumb, I answer, "What do you mean?" I have to almost yell this because we're halfway down the stairs now and the music's bass has picked up so much that my feet are shaking with each descending step.

"Is there something going on with you and Rowen?" He

still has his arm around my shoulders, but it seems like no one has noticed as I scan the room below.

"We're just friends." My subconscious is "*tsking*" at me. As soon as the words pile out of my mouth and float into the atmosphere, I look up. My breath catches as I meet Rowen's cold, hard stare. I almost want to brush Kyle's arm off my shoulders out of instinct, but I have to remember that I'm not taken and I haven't been for two years, due to Rowen. He looks at Kyle and then back at me and I see his fist squeeze the life out of his beer can, causing some wandering eyes to question what just made him act so caveman-ish. It's like everyone in the room knows there's something else going on between us, even if I can't admit it. It takes him less than ten seconds to drop the can on the floor and amble out the front door, slamming it closed.

Kyle's arm slowly lifts off my shoulders. "Friends, my ass." I peer up at him and he chuckles, shaking his head. He walks off to another group of friends and I'm left standing here, looking like I just got caught doing something wrong. But I haven't.

## SIXTEEN

Infuriated. I am so pissed off I can barely see straight. It's such a foreign feeling, I don't typically get angry. Once again, I think it's a pretty useless emotion. But here I am, pissed as all get-out because Rowen just made me look like a complete freaking idiot! I quickly spill it all to Hannah Marie and Anna witnessing Rowen's little fit. The more I ramble, the more pissed I get. The anger is bubbling and sizzling through my veins.

"I'll be back," I say through my fury.

I walk outside and put the poster in Hannah's jeep first, then I search the large, perfectly trimmed yard for a sign of Rowen. I know he's still here because I can see that stupid truck parked at the far end of the corner. I'm going to find him, and I'm going to give him a piece of my mind. *Asshole!*

As soon as I scan the yard for a second time, I see him slowly walking up the paved road. His hands are in his jean pockets and his hat is on backwards. Even from several yards away I can see how tight his shirt is on his biceps and for one, teeny, tiny second, it takes the anger away... but then it quickly comes back as I tread towards him.

Here we are, standing in the middle of the road giving each other a stare down. My stare is definitely laced with anger and is full of emotion whereas his eyes are... empty.

I yell, "What was that about?!"

"What?"

"Don't you play stupid with me, Rowen Michael! You just made everyone in that room stare at me like I was a complete idiot!"

Rowen doesn't say a damn thing. He just stares at me. I can feel his gaze all over my body, taking a bit longer on the skin showing below my shirt. Everywhere his eyes land, I feel the scorching heat left behind.

"Are you into him?" *Oh, Jesus!* This is about jealousy?!

"What if I was?" I cross my arms as he looks down at his feet.

"I don't know." He's so even-tempered and here I am, busting at the freaking seams.

Walking towards him, "What don't you know? Does that bother you? Me being with someone else? Because, that's your fault." I take my finger and push it against his chest. He looks down at my finger touching him and I know I've broken the no-touching rule, but this isn't for fun. I'm just plain angry.

"I know."

"Ugh!" I yell and throw my hands up, turning around to walk a few feet away from him. Why am I so mad? I know I'm acting ridiculous, but I can't seem to get my emotions in check. I'm the most docile person there is and right now I just want to smack him... hard.

"Well?" I ask, as I whip around and face him again, arms still crossed.

"Of course it bothers me." I inhale a sharp breath and feel the nerves wrap around my heart and squeeze. I feel like there is a little snake in my chest, coiling and uncoiling around every heartbeat.

"Why are you so calm? Fight with me!" I yell.

"Why do you want me to fight with you? You've done nothing wrong; I'm in the wrong here and it kills me."

"Because I'm just so angry and I just want to unleash it on you but you're being so calm and I just feel like a moron yelling at you in the middle of the street for next to nothing." My voice has decreased to its normal tone and I can hear the shakiness that has replaced its strong tone.

"Do what you need to do, Sadie. Yell at me, hit me, I don't care. Do whatever you need to do to feel better." My heart hurts. My heart literally hurts staring into his deep brown, golden eyes that are so hollow.

My eyes start to pool at the corners as I whisper, "I want to hate you so bad." I have to choke back a sob clawing at a rapid speed to be unleashed. He takes a few steps toward me, eyeing me to see if I take a step away. I should. I should step back and retreat to the house, snuggle up with Kyle or someone who will make me forget everything, but I stand still. Unmoving.

He takes a few more steps towards me and says, "Just let me make you feel better, please." His voice is desperate and I can't help but let his arms wrap around my tiny frame. Once they do, the tears fall fast. They fall fast and they're intense. Being friends with someone shouldn't be this hard. There's unresolved feelings buried so deep inside me and I don't know what to do with them. It's like I'm this small goldfish swimming in the world's largest ocean, lost and confused surrounded by so many things that can hurt me. The memories, the heartbreak, it's all too much.

Knowing this is pushing the limits of our friendship, I take a step back and wipe my eyes. Not meeting his, not once. I turn my back and walk to the house, wiping my eyes and giving myself a few breathing moments before I go inside and pretend like everything's okay. Like I'm okay.

NEARLY EVERYONE KNOWS about Rowen's and my little spat outside Kyle's party. It's been a week and a half since the party and Rowen and I haven't spoken a single word about it. Hannah and Anna have hounded me on the details but I always change the subject, not wanting to rehash it with anyone, not even myself, and especially not my mother.

"Do you want to talk about the thing with Rowen and you?" I close my eyes and take a deep breath. I don't answer her as we weave through the home décor isles at the store. We're here to shop for some decorations for Alicia's and I's new apartment. It comes fully furnished since it's still on campus, but we both promised each other that we'd pick up some things to spruce it up before school started in full-force.

I pick up a rose gold lamp and place it in the cart, not meeting my mom's stare. I know she means well, but I don't want to talk about it. I feel like an idiot and I feel weak and I've spent the last two years becoming emotionally strong; it's not okay to feel like this... again.

She clears her throat, busying herself with bathroom rugs and I finally speak up. "I don't want to talk about it. We're friends and it's a hard line to balance on after everything. It will just take some time." That's probably the most borderline, non-juicy answer I could give, but... meh. I could really get into all the intricate details of my feelings for Rowen, but she would probably want a licensed therapist to set me straight.

Thankfully, she leaves it alone after my monotone answer and we end up spending entirely too money much on the things for my apartment, and then we top it off with so much food at The Cheesecake Eatery that I'll probably need to buy a bigger size in my lifeguarding suit. I've always loved hanging out with my mom, which is not something most twenty-year old girls can say, but my mom is honestly fun to be around. We've always bonded over back-to-school shopping. I've never been one of those girls who just absolutely lives for shopping but somehow, she's always made it fun. She'd drag me to the mall and we'd feast on those delicious, warm, salty pretzels for "shopping power" and then we'd trail through the mall deciding what I wanted to get. She never really told me no to anything; she's always let me make my own decisions and be my own person. If I wanted to wear neon pink, sparkly shoes paired with a Carolina Panthers light blue jersey and shorts, then she'd let me. She was very adamant about allowing me to become my own person; I just hope she likes the way I ended up.

As we pull up to the driveway laughing about the fact that Dad still hasn't be able to straighten our mailbox (no matter how many times he's tried it always ends up leaning slightly to the left the next day). My mom puts the car in park and places her hand on mine as I reach to unbuckle my seatbelt.

"Wait a second, Sade."

"Okay... Why do you have your serious voice on?" I ask, as she gently releases her warm hand from mine. I sit back in my seat, uncomfortable.

"I want to say something to you and I don't want your dad to overhear." My eyebrows scrunch forward and I'm instantly concerned. My parents are a team; they've never gone behind each other's back to say something to me before, not something important, at least. When I would get a bad grade on a test, they'd both sit me down at our kitchen table and talk to me about it. When my mom had a little cancer scare last year (not to worry, it was a fluke), they both sat me down and told me, so this... is off.

My mom leans back and stares at our house as she begins, "I want to talk to you about Rowen." Before I can say anything, she puts her hand up, palm facing outward, to stop me. "I know your father and I have been telling you to think with your head your entire life and it's been good advice... until now." I look over at her and her eyes are that perfect hazel color, showing the only sentiment, I ever seen in them: comfort. "I know things are weird with you and Rowen and there's a lot at play, and if you think with your head, like we've taught you to do, I don't think... " She pauses and I watch her scan my entire face. "I think you need to think with your heart, on this one, Sadie." I stare at her for a few minutes, then look away, not wanting her to see the emotions playing all over my face. "Ignoring what your heart says won't lead you to happiness. Trust me." She scoffs a little. "I tried to ignore my heart once, and I ended up in a place that I didn't want to be— leading me to a lot of hurt. The moment I listened to my heart again, though, it all clicked." I look over at her again and she's giving me a tiny smile as she reaches for my hands clenched in my lap.

"No one's made you smile the way Rowen used to, and there may be another Rowen out there for you but if you keep ignoring what your heart says, you're never going to find him." I bite my bottom lip, to stop the trembling. I guess I'm not that good at hiding my feelings from everyone.

"I think you need to take some time and shut the world out for a bit. Shut out everything but that huge, perfect heart of yours, and listen to it. Figure out what you want and be happy." I give her a small smile and softly nod my head. But, what she doesn't understand is that my heart isn't so perfect anymore; it's scarred and jagged and if I listen to it, I know exactly where it's going to lead me. It's going to lead me down a path that I'm not sure I want to walk down again.

## SEVENTEEN

I know the time is coming. The clock is ticking loudly in my brain, chanting "talk to Rowen" with every freaking chime. We still haven't discussed the epic stare-down followed by my floodgates bursting open, drowning everyone in sight. It's been more than strained between the two of us, and during the past two weeks at work, we've kept our distance. He still waits by his truck after my shift, but we never say more than a few words to each other. It's taunting in every way possible and draining for me to keep my guard up. It's like neither of us knows what to say. It's obvious we're both hoping for a way out of all the pressure... and we're soon to get it since I leave for school in exactly eight days. That leaves eight days to get our shit together and figure out if we're gonna make it as friends, or not.

When I went to the Animal Adoption Festival yesterday, I met up with Hannah Marie and Anna, who also brought along a huge group of our friends. Kyle was there, but kept his distance, still sticking to his story of not wanting to get caught in the crossfire of Rowen and I. Then there were a few stragglers that I vaguely remember from high school and of course... the bright red cherry on top: Rowen. We broke off a shameless piece of tension between the two of us by including each other in group-wide conversation, but it was epically awkward and every one could sense it. Long pauses after we'd talk, long stares until we'd catch each other, and then a touch of whiplash in an attempt to look away. Fun times!

Part of me wants to just take Alicia's advice and either: 1. Have sex with some random guy to see if I can become somewhat emotionally attached to someone else, or 2. Just call Rowen up and talk to him about things; see what he has to say. I definitely will be going with the latter of those choices, as I don't think I'm ready to strip down naked in front of some guy and bare my soul to them. I've only ever had sex with Rowen, which in Alicia's eyes, is half my issue. I recognize all the warning signs, I get it. The only person I've had sex with is Rowen and that was two years ago. Can you dry up at the age of twenty? Surely not... right? Regardless of my sex life, or lack thereof, I need to make a move to fix things before I leave; I know that. But, I think I'll wait until the very last moment... that way I can use the year buffer to my advantage.

My parents are gone for the day. Mom at the elementary school volunteering and Dad at his back-to-school meeting, so it gives me plenty of time to "shut the world out", per the motherly advice I got earlier this week. What better way to do that than lying facedown on our oversized leather couch and letting my heart and mind engage into World War Three? I half want to put on some ACDC jams to build up the momentum of fists flying, hair pulling, and all-around wrestling, but I don't. I let the silence of the room overcome my senses, and before long, I'm dead asleep. Only to be woken up by a persistent pounding on my front door.

"Jesus!" I spring up from the leather couch, face peeling away with the sticky backing, and instantly reach to make sure my skin is still there. I can feel the subtle ruggedness of my scar so I know that I still, in fact, have a face. I give the couch a dirty look and vaguely remember the pounding that woke me up. I tip-toe over to the door, peep through the tiny hole, and see nothing. Did I dream it?

Regaining my bearings, I walk over to the kitchen, checking around the house for anything abnormal, glancing at the clock. It's only been a few hours, and my plan of figuring out what the hell to do with Rowen has already gone to shit. I shut the world out a little too much, apparently. Reaching inside our cabinet, I grab a glass of water and fill it up to the brim, chugging it in one drink. I stare out the window, and nostalgia takes me by the ponytail and yanks me to all the memories I've had out in that front yard. The grass is its brightest green right now due to the North Carolina summer weather. The bark on the giant oak tree towards the road is its deepest brown, limbs swaying in the summer breeze. It's a perfect day outside, and I swim in the fact that my life is pretty damn good. Sure, I've had some unfortunate stuff happen, but in reality, I have a good life. Yes, things are unfinished with Rowen, but let's get real: it's not the end of the world... right?

"Wait, what?" I mutter, looking past the skyscraper of a tree. I instantly drop the glass in the sink, hearing it clatter against the aluminum entirety. Just beyond the oak tree, parked on my quiet street, is a sleek black Camaro SS with bright blue stripes lining the sides. I peek around the yard, looking for the one person that I know owns that vehicle. I feel a chill race up my spin and I run over to the old cream-colored phone still attached to the wall with a spiraling cord. I yank it off its receiver and dial the one number I pretend not to know, but really, the numbers are embedded into my brain in a gold sparkling color—flashing rapidly, as if they're saying, "We never left!"

He answers on the first ring.

"Sadie?"

"Rowen," I say, all breathy.

"What's wrong?!" I can hear the worry in his tone.

"I think Mark is at my house." My eyes dart from the kitchen window to the front door, wondering if he's just going to barge in here at any moment.

"*What?* I'm coming over now. I'm only a few streets away." I hear a bell chime in the background and I know he's probably at the one tiny market we have downtown.

*Wait! Why did I call Rowen? What?!*

"Wait, Rowen. It's probably fine. I don't even know why I called you. Mark is like a sweet little puppy." A very attached puppy.

"I'm comin'." He says and I hear the rumble of his truck starting up. "Do not hang up the phone, Sadie." He says this possessively and if I'm being honest, I can feel it all the way to my core.

"Okay." I answer. There is only silence on the other end of the line. I listen hard to the background noises, only to distract myself from fully combusting. I can't believe I called Rowen. My mind thought "DANGER!" and I called Rowen. What does that say?

"*Shit!*" I whisper as I hear the banging on my front door again.

"Don't you dare hang up. I'm almost there."

I take a deep breath, letting the air fully fill my lungs. "Rowen, I'm serious. He is harmless. A little bit excessive but he's probably the type of guy that cries after sex." I nervously giggle and feel my heart speed up. My hands start to tremble as the adrenaline of the pounding door starts to ricochet though my house.

"Hold on. This is ridiculous!" Despite Rowen's protests, I let go of the phone, letting it hang and twirl around against the wall. I'm a big girl; I can handle Mark. He really is like a tiny fly, annoying but harmless.

I whip open the front door, welcoming the summer scent. "What the hell are you doing here, Mark?" I yell, fully annoyed at this moment. Part of me feels bad that he is this hung-up on me. We literally only kissed a handful of times, and, they sucked. So emotionless.

"Sadie. I want to talk to you!" His voice is strained and I can't help but chuckle at his attempt.

"How did you even find out where I lived?" I close my front door behind me and lean against it, putting the necessary space between the two of us. He looks so prim and proper: his blonde hair parted down the side and gelled impeccably, like it's a sculpture that belongs in a museum.

"I remembered it from your license." He says this with such a proudness.

"When did you see my license?" I gulp.

"That night at Shellby's. When you went to the bathroom and paid with your credit card. They had to see your license, remember?" Yes, I remember clearly. He made me pay for my OWN food on a DATE! I ended it soon after that, friends.

"You need to leave, Mark. I'm not interested in you. At all." I look dead into his crystal blue eyes, hoping that I reach some part of his detached mind. He looks like a sad puppy. Like I've just taken away his bone.

He reaches for me and I squish up against my door, the warm paint pressed against my bare shoulders. His fingers grasp onto my hand, squeezing them just enough to be persistent. I try to whip my hand back but he only holds on tighter. He may he harmless and much smaller than Rowen in the muscle department, but he still exceeds my tiny frame in every way possible. My head snaps up to the end of my street where I see a rusty ol' Dodge swinging around the corner. I can almost feel the rumbling of the engine in my limbs. Rowen is in my driveway and out of his truck in five seconds, flat. No, seriously. I wish I had a stopwatch.

"Get off of her!" he yells hoarsely, and my eyes almost fall out of their sockets! Before I know what's happening, Rowen has Mark in a headlock lying right on top of my mom's holly bush! Little red berries flying off in different directions and it looks like two cats are brawling with one another.

"Rowen! Stop!" I yell, although Mark's girly screams are outweighing my voice. I watch for a few more moments before I finally take the plunge and grab Rowen's arm. He pauses the second I do, looking down at my bare hand clenched on his forearm. It's amazing how tiny my hand looks splayed on his arm.

"Stop!" I beg, and his face is almost trembling. His strong jaw that was clenched seconds ago loosens, just as his bloody fist does. He looks directly into my pleading face and finally gives up. He sits back on his butt and scoots away from Mark, who is full-on crying. I mean, I can actually see tears rolling down his face. The phrase "blood and tears" has a whole new meaning to me now.

The second he sees Rowen scoot away from him, he stands up and sprints to his car. He screams, "You and your boyfriend are CRAZY!" I laugh out loud as he barrels into his Camaro and squeals down the road so fast that he ignores the stop sign. Once he is out of sight, I plop down on the ground, beside Rowen. I can hear his rapid breathing in an attempt to calm himself down. I just watched an entirely different Rowen come to life: one full of rage and fury.

"I'm sorry," he says, but it comes out like a ghost's whisper. I crouch in-between his perched-up legs, feeling the sidewalk scrape at my knees, and bring his face to mine. The second I do, my heart crumbles. Emotions are etched all over his formed face. His eyes are filled with tears, and his full bottom lip is trembling. It's so bizarre seeing such a strong-bodied man like Rowen look so incredibly defeated.

We stare at each other's faces until I see the tears spilling from his eyes. Without hesitation, I crush his head against my body, letting him fall apart in my arms. Blindsided by this, I have to choke back my own sob.

He rambles, "I'm sorry. I'm so sorry. I saw him and a look of fear in your eyes and I was back in that moment with the robber... " He pauses and I sit back on my legs, "I, I should have saved you two years ago." I gulp so loudly that the birds flying high above us probably heard it.

"Rowen, stop feeling guilty for that. I've told you before, there was nothing you could have done to stop what happened."

In between sniffles, he looks up at me and takes in my expression. His face is tear-stained, and in that moment, I realize just how hurt the both of us are over what happened. There's just so much pain intertwined in the two of us that I picture wicked, thorn infested vines sprouting from the ground, wrapping their lengthy arms around the pair of us. Neither of us want to move, and I suddenly have the urge to kiss away every tear spilling down his face. I want the entire past to be erased, I want to start over in this very moment.

"How do you expect me to fully forgive you, if you can't forgive yourself?"

He takes a few minutes to answer, voice rough and scratchy. "I don't know... I really don't know."

We stay wrapped in each other's arms on our little

concrete pad for what seems like hours until he gets the nerve to stand up to wipe the blood off his knuckles. My heart is out-of-control in my chest as I stand and stare at his body, his shirt taut around his back, his jeans hugging every curve. My heart is slowly losing its battle between it and my mind.

"I think we need to talk... " I say, and he turns around looking overcome. He nods his head in agreement.

He opens his mouth, not meeting my face. "Tomorrow, after work. We'll go somewhere and talk." I listen to his feet scraping the concrete as he walks down to his truck. I watch him back all the way out of my driveway before I bow my head and let the emotional roller coaster take off.

## EIGHTEEN

The smell of a fresh summer rain fills my nose as I climb out of my car, rounding the back side to get to Rowen's parked truck. He's parked it to the very brim of Old Man Henry's tallest hill, sitting on the bed, with his bare legs dangling. He doesn't meet my presence as I climb up, but I'm fully aware that our knees mere inches apart.

For a while, we both just stare out at the landscape. Green, grassy hills flow on top of one another for miles and miles. I can tell they've just been mowed because their grassy shreds are still freshly laid out upon green floor—the smell of grass floats in the air and if I concentrate hard enough, I can almost smell the nightly moon, too. The sun has just barely set and the stars are soon to be approaching, casting that perfect picture-worthy, romantic light over our bodies. Being out here brings back a wave of nostalgia. This is Rowen's and my spot; the first time he kissed me, we were here. The first time we had sex, where I lost my virginity, it was out here in his truck bed, the stars being our only witness. This is where everything started. This is where I fell in love with him.

"So... " he says, interrupting the symphony of crickets in the distance.

"So... " I say back, unable to really form words. I know I need to lay everything out in the open and that we need to come to some sort of a conclusion, but now that I'm here, I'm at a loss.

"Sorry about yesterday... I just lost it." I can see out of the corner of my eye that he has his head bent low, like he's ashamed. "I saw you there, vulnerable again, and I just acted."

I nod my head in understanding. I get it. "I understand. It seems that the attack didn't just affect me. I sometimes forget that you were there, too." Guilt seems to be filling my mind more and more these days.

"I think our breakup affected me more than the actual attack, and that's all on me. It's my fault."

"Rowen," I say, and he turns his head and looks at me. "Being your friend kind of sucks."

For a moment, his eyebrows dip and then he grins, and I let out an audible laugh, which he soon follows. "Back at ya, sport." We laugh a little longer and I'm thankful for the lightness in this moment. It's refreshing from how it normally feels, like we're trapped in this dark subdued place, all the time. It's like, give me a damn flashlight!

"It's not working. At least it isn't for me." I murmur, looking back out at all the expanding hills.

"So then, what do we do?"

I don't say anything for a while, trying to collect my thoughts and calm down my erratic breathing. The thought of this being our last conversation, this being our goodbye, makes me want to reach over and cling to him for dear life... and that urge does nothing but scare me. My heart is too invested in him to make any decisions... this woodsy scent eloping with my senses, his rough voice filling my ears, his knee brushing against mine... it's too much. So, I do the only thing I can think of.

"I have a proposition for you." My heart soars, as my mind balks.

"Are you using my own tactics on me?" He lets out a chuckle and I swear I can feel it inside my chest.

"I think we take the year, to figure out what we want. I need to get myself together. I... I don't know what I want. But being friends with you is just too much."

He takes a second to take in the landscape, which gives me a perfect excuse to study his strong profile. "So, what you're saying is that it's all or nothing?" Our faces meet and the shadowed crevices give nothing away.

"Yes," I breathe. "It's either we try this thing between us again, or we're done."

"I already know what I want," he says in a husky voice as he adjusts the hat that's perched perfectly on the back of his head. "I want you. All of you. So, the chess pieces are in your hands."

I swallow loudly, squeezing my eyes shut and clenching my jaw. What am I doing?! My mouth opens, propelling words faster than my mind and stop me. "Well, if I decide I want to try us again, then I'll come back to the Club... again. If I don't, then I'll find something else and put the necessary distance between us." Because, distance is exactly what I'll need if I decide I can't be with him. If I can't get my heart and mind to come to an agreeance, I'm going to need about fifteen hundred football fields separating us. Right now, it feels as if I'm at an impasse.

He says nothing, but slowly nods his head. Then he peeks up at me, the moon casting a flawless glow on his face, emphasizing those devious shadows along all the right places. I feel my hand twitch to touch him. "So, no communication, right? Just like last year?"

"Exactly," I answer. I won't be able to make a decision if I talk to him. I'll be swayed by his voice, his presence. I just know it. He might as well be a damn vampire.

For a while, we just sit on the bed of his truck. Staring at the distance, lost in our own thoughts. I glance up and watch the stars twinkle in the sky and a state of calmness washes over me. It feels so right to be here, under these same stars with him. How can something that feels so right, be so wrong?

"Ya know... " he starts, as he looks over at me and then back at the midnight sky. "It's like the stars have realigned, just for us." My eyes saunter toward him and then back to the sparkle above. If I look closely enough, they really have...

"I feel like we have bad luck," I whisper, still staring at the sky.

"There's no such thing." He leans back on his hands. "There's just... luck. It's all about how you look at it."

My expression stays the same, wondering what he means, and he starts up again. "Think of the attack. You could look at it as bad luck, but you could also look at it as good luck. It turned you into a badass, strong-willed girl. I think that's a good thing."

I take in his profile again, not caring if he catches me. I take in the entirety of his face. Everything so perfectly placed. His cheek bones prominent like his jaw. A perfectly straight nose that leads down to luscious lips. I watch as he brings his head down from the sky and turns towards me. "Samantha being a devious, lying bitch... that could be considered bad luck, but you could also look at is as good luck; now you know what a real friend is like. There's always two parts to every-thing. Just like with luck."

"Are there two parts to what happened with us?" I

counter, barely audible. I bite my lip while waiting for his answer. His eyes dip down to my lips and back up to my eyes.

"Yeah, it's not bad luck. It just made us both realize that what we had was real." My heart blooms at his words but my mind has her fists up, ready to guard. What an interesting thing to leave me with all year to dissect.

For the next hour, we sit back and talk like old friends. Reminiscing over the memories, our friends, all the things we did together before everything went to hell. It all feels so familiar and so comforting to be in this place with him again. Away from all the hurt and emotions usually swarming the two of us; it almost makes me regret setting up this proposition because suddenly, being away from him for the entire school year feels like getting a swift kick to the gut.

"We should probably go. Old Man Henry's gonna come out here with a shotgun soon." I crack up at his words. That happened one time, when Rowen and I were out here for hours. Literally hours. We had sex (a couple of times, to be honest), danced to the staticky country music pouring out of his crappy truck speakers. Then we laid in the grass, holding hands. It was probably one of the best nights of my life, until Old Man Henry came out with a shotgun, threatening to shoot us "kids." Rowen and I jumped into his truck, laughing uncontrollably and he sped down the dirt road as fast as he could. Dust was flying everywhere, but in the distance I could see a determined overweight man with a shotgun perched on his shoulder.

I laugh. "You're right. Let's go." The goodbye is looming in the air and my laughing stops within seconds. I hop down from his truck, brushing the debris from my bare legs. He jumps down beside me, landing softly in the grass, and I cannot breathe. Not a single breath is leaving my body. We're only standing a few feet apart, and I watch as his chest rises and falls unsteadily.

"Bye, Rowen," I whisper, quickly turning around and forcing my heavy feet in the direction of my parked car. Before I get another foot away from him, his hand grabs mine from behind. I freeze in my spot, allowing the grass to tickle my ankles. I take a deep breath as he sharply pulls me back into his presence. For a second, it sounds like the crickets have ceased chirping, the cicadas stopped humming in the hollows of the trees... it's as if the stars really have realigned, just for us. In this moment, the world is quiet. Just Rowen and I.

He takes his hands and grabs the sides of my head, bringing us face-to-face. I feel the patchy calluses on his hands, more than likely from the gym, as they scratch my high cheek bones. His fingers intertwine in my chlorine-scented waves as he tips my face up to the point that I can feel his breath on my nose. "I need you to know," he whispers, lips so close that I can almost feel their softness. "That I want you, Sadie. So. Fucking. Bad." My eyes widen, as I feel my lips moving even closer to his. Just one more centimeter, and they'll be on mine. This will all be over. I want him to kiss me. I want to feel his lips brush against mine, I want to feel the hunger that I see in his brown depths. I want him to make the world stop spinning on its very axis. I close my eyes, imagining what would happen if I just did it. If I just leaned in a fraction of a second and pressed my lips against his. Would the world cease to exist? Would I cease to exist? Would it erase every single tear in my heart?

"I want you... and I usually get what I want." His voice is pure sex, husky and strained, making me tremble all over. Standing this close, breathing his air, has my chest rising faster than it ever has before. Rowen tensely backs away from me, unwrapping his tangled fingers. I hear the ground crushing under his feet as treads around to his truck. I stay put, only a few feet from the bed. My body jumps to the sound of his truck door rattling. The engine revs up, making the grass floor shake beneath my legs. I watch as his headlights fade away under the expanding hills, and I finally let out a breath that I wasn't aware I was holding. I consciously reach up and place my warm fingers on my mouth, rubbing my lips back and forth, painfully slow. I want to know what it feels like to have his skillful lips on mine again. I want to hear that husky, throaty voice groan as we connect once more. I want his mouth on every single part of my body, giving me that tingly feeling on my most intimate parts. I want it all. I want him. I want him back.

PART THREE

SUMMER, 2012

# NINETEEN

I'm almost positive that every other twenty-year old knows how to use social media, everyone but ME! Did you really think that I could go the entire school year without checking in on Rowen? I tried. I tried my hardest to just simply put him out of my mind. I dated. I even got naked with a guy, but there was Rowen... right there in the back of my mind with his smoldering gaze, backwards hat, and perfectly long lashes covering those deep brown eyes. Ugh.

When I couldn't take it anymore, when I'd reached my limit, I very deviously used Alicia's profile (she really shouldn't leave it open on her computer) and tried to search for Rowen. I got flustered after about three seconds and ended up rebooting her computer... oops. So, here I am. A year later and I haven't even gotten a tiny sliver of intel on Rowen, other than fishing information out of Kyle (very innocently, I might add).

"Alicia, hurry the hell up!" I squeeze my head out from my car window. She briefly puts her own head out of our miniscule, crappy, bottom-floor apartment and flips me the bird. I laugh under my breath. Alicia is literally late for everything. Class? She's late. Lunch date? Late. A frat party? She shows up two hours after she said she'd be there. She's relentless when it comes to not being on time. It drives me absolutely up-the-wall, considering I'm early for everything, almost annoyingly early.

I think Alicia and I are the last ones on campus. It's sparse. Barely any cars parked in the student parking lot, no professors walking around carelessly with their heads buried in their phones, nothing. Just me waiting on Alicia. I was halfway home when she called me, asking to stay the night at my house. She was just going to stay in the empty apartment for the night, then her mom was going to pick her up in the morning, but the one thing I truly know about Alicia is that she hates to be alone so I turned my tiny Ford around and came back to get her.

A few weeks ago, Alicia's car blew up, literally. I was with her, so that was fun. We were on our way home from getting Chinese off-campus at this little hole-in-the-wall restaurant that sells fake purses on the side, when all of a sudden, I noticed smoke pouring from below the hood of her car. She pulled over, gravel crunching beneath her tires, and we barreled out of our seats (still clutching the Chinese food, of course). The second we got out of the car, it caught fire. I guess she didn't realize that you had to actually put oil in your car to make it go, so there's that. She blames it on the fact that she doesn't have a father figure in her life ... she said, "Aren't dads supposed to do these things for you? I don't have one." The tow truck driver rolled his wrinkled eyes at her, then smiled; he had some type of tobacco sticking in his teeth, and his longing stare at Alicia's model-like olive-colored bare legs was enough to have me call one of our other friends to come pick us and our Chinese up on the side of the road.

"Come help me!" I hear Alicia say from the doorway. She

has three pink crates in her arms that are piled up higher than her head, blocking her face, and she has three bags strapped around her body.

"Oh my God. You're a mess," I say, through a fit of laughter as I skip up to her full hands and help her load the car.

Halfway down the highway, she finally turns down our mini ACDC concert and says, "I'm literally so excited to stay at your house. It's like we're having a slumber party."

"We have a slumber party every night. We live together," I counter, keeping my eyes on the fast cars zipping around us.

"I know, but this is different. I get to hang at your childhood home; I get to see where you grew up. And... " She trails off, bringing her hand up to her chin and tapping it repeatedly. "And maybe I get to see Rowen."

I almost bring the car to a slamming stop, my foot teetering over the brake. "There is no way you're seeing Rowen tonight. I haven't even see him, or told him... " I waiver from the last part because I'm still feeling all wonky from my decision. She pouts, so I add, "You should come back for our friend, Kyle's, annual 4th of July party. That way you can meet everyone."

She nods her head in an excited manner, smiling from ear to ear. She turns the music back up and leaves me to my thoughts of Rowen.

This whole year, I've tested out every possible way to get Rowen out of my system. I dated two guys, and I mean, like... really dated. Not another Marky-Mark situation, who by the way, transferred to another school. Apparently, Rowen scared him that much. Anyway, boyfriend number one, was one that I met in the library. He kept staring at me from several tables away, making my face flush with every passing second. I finally got the nerve to walk over to him, because I simply couldn't concentrate. I asked him what he was staring at. I still had Mark fresh in my mind and my bodyguard, aka Rowen, was over a hundred miles away, so I was not in the mood to feature in someone's library fantasy. When I spoke in a bold voice, holding my stare to his, he grinned at me. A little tiny part of his full lip tipped up on the right side, casting a dimple just below his cheek, and I smiled out of reaction. He replied, "I'm staring at you because you're hard *not* to stare at. Haven't you noticed every guy in this room staring at you?" I remembered looking around the quiet library and people's eyes really were lingering on us. I felt my body break out into a fevered sweat.

The rest is basically history. He asked me out and I agreed. We went on a few dates to some of the restaurants that weren't too far away from campus, we went to some home football games, it was all very casual and easy. But I learned a long time ago that easy also means boring. Love is difficult, relationships are difficult; it shouldn't necessarily be easy and calming. I want to feel something. I want to feel exhilarated. I want to feel those butterflies that Rowen gave me the first time he held my hand. I needed to feel something other than my impending thoughts of him. So, I ended it with boyfriend number one. It was all on good terms; I think he knew we were better as friends.

Then there was boyfriend number two; who I refer as "freak in the sheets" but his real name is Hoyt. "Professor" Hoyt. I made a complete fool out of myself the first time I met him because I addressed him as such in front of my entire Romantic Literature class. When I called him Professor Hoyt, the entire class snickered—causing a pretty crimson shade of red to creep onto my neck and face. He smiled at me gently and said, "You've given me a boost of confidence, but I'm not a professor. I'm just a TA filling in for the first three weeks of class, but thanks." Then he winked at me and I felt a familiar pull in my stomach. He was attractive, and smart. He had jet black hair, and crystal blue eyes. He wore those fancy dress shirts with ties and slacks that hugged all the right spots. I often found myself daydreaming about him when he would talk of Jane Austen and his all-time favorite, Byron. I would catch him looking in my direction and he'd give me a small smile, barely playing at his lips. I'm sure no one else noticed, but I did and I liked the way it made me feel. Almost as if it was a drug. I couldn't get enough of him. It took my mind off Rowen for 0.3 seconds, too, and I appreciated that. At soon as the three weeks were over, he came right up to my chair as I was shoving my MacBook in my leather-bound Fossil bag, and asked me out. I agreed, nodding my head wildly, holding back the biggest smile.

He was older than me, nearing twenty-five and working on his Master's degree, and it was a breath of fresh air. I went straight from boyish Rowen, to creeper Mark, to fake boyfriend Rowen who beats up creepy guys named Mark, to library boy (who didn't elicit a single spark in me), and then I landed Hoyt. He took me on real dates, and I felt like I was actually in my twenties. The first restaurant he took me to was a fancy sushi one, and we had a really good time. I felt sexy and like I had my life together when I pulled on my red dress, the one that hit right at my mid-thigh. The push-up bra I had stashed away in the back of my underwear drawer made my boobs look as if I was in my mid-twenties instead of barely reaching adulthood. I remember the exact moment Hoyt saw me in that dress. His eyes roamed the entirety of my body, making me feel the need to clench my legs together. His look rocked me to my core.

The date was simply perfect. We laughed at my attempt to eat sushi; I embarrassingly gagged on the raw, slimy fish, so he ended up taking me to get some gelato to end the night. We shared bites from one another and I would curse myself for wanting to wrap my mouth around something other than his plastic spoon. His crystal blue eyes were as bright as the sky on a sunny day. I got lost in them that night more than I care to admit.

Things went slow at first. I was like a little schoolgirl when he would sometimes wait for me after my classes, just to walk me to my next destination. We would text back and forth while I was back home, visiting my parents for the holidays. Then BOOM, things went south during spring break.

The weather that day was impeccable. It wasn't too hot or humid, a small breeze rustling the giant oak tree's limbs out front. I was on my knees, burying my hands in dirt, helping my mom plant the yellow and orange marigolds just beneath the windows when I felt a strange need to look towards the road. I wish I hadn't because the second I caught a glimpse of that rusty red fender, my stomach clenched. My breath caught and just like that, I was back at Old Man Henry's, feeling Rowen's hands on my face; telling me he wanted me. He didn't drive down my street. He just sat at the crossroads, parked by the stop signs, truck rumbling in the background. I couldn't see his eyes, I was too far away but I knew it was him. I knew he could see me; just as I could see him. A horn blared from behind him, making me jolt out of my skin. I turned away just as he drove off, and things were never the same again between Hoyt and I.

I tried to ignore it for awhile, the guilt crowding my brain like gnat on a rotten banana. I even rushed us to the next level, finally taking the plunge, moving past all the foreplay that Hoyt was so damn good at. Sex. We had sex, mind-blowing, toe-curling sex but things came to a crashing halt. No pumping the brakes; we came to a tire-squealing, whiplash-inducing stop. I learned two things after having sex with Hoyt. Number one: Sex in my twenties is more pleasurable than in my teens. I think I've reached a sexual high. There is a reason I refer to him as "freak in the sheets". That was all very good, but then came number two: Sex with Hoyt may be epically pleasurable but I felt nothing in my heart for him. He was exciting, and he was definitely skilled with his mouth and hands, but I felt nothing (other than the handful of orgasms). So, I made my decision. I broke things off with Hoyt, shortly after we had sex. I realized that I better start listening to my incredibly determined heart and give this whole thing with Rowen another go around. After all, if I can say goodbye to Hoyt, who no doubt is a sex god from another life, all because of Rowen... that has to mean something. Right?

GLANCING IN THE REARVIEW MIRROR, listening to Alicia yammer on and on about my house and how it looks so "cozy," I fix my hair into a messy bun perched high on my head. I take my sunglasses off, wiping the layer of grease off my face and smile at my scar. It's barely there anymore, thanks to the overly priced scar removal cream that my mom sends to me in care packages. I wonder if it bothers her more than it bothers me?

I just knew my mom would make an enormous dinner when Alicia and I made it home. Any chance she has to celebrate, she will. Tonight, we're celebrating that Alicia and I are now seniors and that it was Alicia's first time staying at my house. The night flew by: dinner with my parents who didn't stop talking the second we sat down to gobble up some home-cooked pot roast and veggies, then Alicia went through all my high school yearbooks, stopping at every hot guy's picture, raising her eyebrows and after that we watched a chick flick. We ended the night binging on my mom's homemade, choco- latey, mouth-watering brownies, all while kicking each other in my tiny full-sized bed.

Alicia's mom picked her up an hour before I had to head into the country club and I was as nervous as a snowman in July. I didn't have a plan with seeing Rowen. I was just going to show up and hope he'd understand that this was me accepting to be his girlfriend, or at least to try things for awhile. I didn't tell my parents, I was twenty (almost twenty- one). I was an adult, but somehow being back in my childhood home for the third summer in a row, I felt like I was still a little girl with pigtails who needs permission to leave the house. Especially, to go meet up with Rowen. But regardless, I am an adult and I don't need their permission to date Rowen.

The second I step out my car and am greeted with the stark whiteness of the country club building, the faint smell of chlorine fills my nose and I am at ease. This will be my third year working here and each year it feels a little more like home. With Sash's aviators and his mumbling about the bratty kids, Morgan's and my swims during break, and Hallie's sneaking of snacks out of the concessions, it all feels familiar and it sets the butterflies swarming in my stomach at ease.

I slowly walk up to the iron gate and swing it open, feeling my heart thump in my chest. I look around for Rowen and I don't see him. I could have sworn I saw his truck parked in the parking lot, but maybe I made that part up. What if he doesn't come back? Maybe he thought we shouldn't be together... what will I do? I can literally already feel my heart cracking vehemently, which scares me right out of my red bathing suit. We aren't even a thing yet and I'm already afraid he's going to destroy me again.

Just as I'm rounding the corner, I see Sash's tall, lengthy

body standing with his back to me, talking to someone. I quickly peer my head around his frame, and then I see him. As soon as I spot the chocolatey brown hair flipping out from behind his hat, the butterflies pick up their pace. I smile as his eyes form into saucers. In the middle of Sash's sentence, Rowen steps away from him; I can hear Sash's colorful curses but all I'm focused on is Rowen. It's amazing what one year can do to someone. He looks mostly the same, except his muscles have more tone to them. A perfect V-shaped torso leading down to his red swim trunks. I can only hope that I look different, too; I feel different. Everything feels different. I'm more aware of things than last year... like the way my stomach is already clenching in anticipation that I just might have Rowen's lips on mine.

When he rounds Sash's body, he's standing spitting distance away from me. He raises his dark eyebrows as if he's asking me to confirm that I'm actually here. I slowly shrug my shoulders and give him a tiny grin, trying to hide my giddiness. He breaks out into a heart-stopping smile, flashing those perfectly white teeth, and comes even closer to me, telling Sash to shut up.

"Is this what I think it means?" he asks, crossing his arms over his exposed chest.

I don't answer right away; I kind of like seeing him squirm (insert evil laugh here). "I guess... " And my lips tip upward.

"We've got a date tomorrow night, after work. And tell your parents you're busy for your birthday." My eyebrows scrunch together in confusion but on the inside, I'm doing actual cartwheels.

"You already have stuff planned?" I quip.

"Yes." His darkened eyes meet mine.

I brush my long brown hair behind my shoulder and cross

my arms. "Someone was a little cocky that I'd return this summer... "

Rowen only winks at me, giving me that grin. The one that if I were wearing panties, they'd totally be on the concrete floor in between my legs. He walks backwards to take his stand at his lifeguarding station and I do the same. Avoiding how Sash's aviators are now perched on his nose, eyeing me from above, and Morgan's long blonde hair, gripped in her fist—her eyes wide and mouth open. I smirk to myself and get to work.

# TWENTY

I've been imagining my date with Rowen since the second he told me. It's all I think about. I finally broke down and told my mom, and only my mom. I very bluntly said, "Rowen and I are starting up again," and waited for a knee-jerk reaction but she simply acted nonchalant about it. She isn't fooling me, though; I can see right through her armor. She's happy, but scared, too; a mirror of my own feelings. I'm excited, exhilarated, happy, and all of the above, but there's that little devil on my shoulder crossing her arms, staring daggers into the side of my ear. The angel on the other shoulder, she's basically flying from elatedness.

When I pull up to work, I'm confused when I don't see Rowen's truck parked out front. I guess he might not be working today, but I thought he was. When I glance down at my phone, avoiding a near run-in with the fence, I see a text from him.

**Rowen:** Can't wait for tonight.

I'm swooning. I'm swooning over a simple text. I feel like

I'm back in high school. I quickly text him back, to ease my curiosity.

**Me:** Where are you? Are you not working today?

He texts me back within seconds.

**Rowen:** No, I'm only part-time at the club. I'm working with the football program at the high school for college credit.

I nod my head, although he can't see me. Rowen has always been all about sports. When he first moved to this small town his junior year he was completely bummed that our school didn't have a hockey program. I didn't know him my junior year, but he later confided in me that he was angry for the entire year he was here because of it. He didn't want to move, not one bit, but his parents needed to relocate to help out with his grandpa's illness. Once things between us started to grow, Rowen started to come out of his shell a little, getting more into the sports that our school did offer. But anyway, last I heard, he was going to UNC for physical education or something along those lines. I guess I never really found out what he was in school for after his sudden disappearance three years ago. I didn't really care to know, but, now I want to know. I want to know everything there is to Rowen; I want to relearn his dreams, ambitions, goals. I want to relearn what makes him happy, I want to re-learn everything about him. I want my heart to soar again.

When Rowen's truck pulls up after work, my heart does three backflips, two frontflips, and a roundabout on the bars; that's how anxious I am. The second he opens his door and climbs out, I take a whiff of his scent. I could bathe in it. I want to bottle it up and douse my pillow in it.

Rowen looks particularly striking with his plain black shirt that fits snugly around his arms but more loosely around his waist. His shorts come just to the knee and he even took the notion of not wearing his backwards hat, letting those brown waves shine. My mouth goes dry at the sight of him. I am in such a daze that I don't even realize he is standing a few feet away from me.

I feel like a complete idiot. My hair is wet and smelling of chlorine since I took a few dives with Morgan on our last break. I'd thrown on a little sundress, but my skin feels dry, regardless of the coconut lotion I'd rubbed on my legs.

"Hi," I whisper, gazing upward to meet his over six-foot height.

"Hey, are you ready?" he asks, with a small smile playing at his full lips.

"Yeah, I guess. I feel like an idiot. You look all... perfect and here I am with wet hair, smelling like a pool." I laugh nervously.

"You... " He grabs my hand and I trail after him as he pulls me to the passenger side of his truck, "You look perfect, Sadie." I smile a little as he opens the door up for me and I climb inside, feeling the vinyl seat on my bare legs. I run my right hand over its sticky smooth feeling and hum inside. So many memories, so many memories just from feeling a truck's seat.

The conversation is short lived once Rowen gets in the car and starts to drive to wherever we're going. We're both nervous, and you can tell by the feeling in the air. I bet if he turned the roaring engine off, Mrs. Betty who announces that she's deaf in one ear anytime anyone passes by her front stoop could hear both of our hearts beating erratically. I honestly think I'm more nervous about this date with him than I was on our actual first date.

To break the little neurons floating around our bodies, I ask where we're going.

He doesn't take his eyes off the road. He only grins, "It's a surprise."

Once we pull up to our old high school, and he turns in, I look at him with a perplexed look. The high school? What? He pulls his truck up slowly to the fenced in field and hops out, leaving the truck running. I watch as he unlocks the gate and pushes it wide open. He jumps back in the truck, without looking in my direction and pulls his truck onto the blacktop track. After we get over the few humps of the track, we pull into the ever-expanding green grass football field. I take the field in with one large gaze. When you're up in the stands, the field looks ginormous. It looks huge as guys with big pads on their shoulders are running down to the end zone with a brown football in their hands but now that I'm on the actual field, it's not that big. It seems normal-sized.

"What are we doing here, Rowen?" I say as he backs the truck up to the middle of the field, facing the goal posts.

"Don't you remember?" he says, as he looks over at me. I bite my lip and take a look around. "This is the first place we met. Right there... " He squints his eyes, causing wrinkles at their sides and I follow where his finger is pointing. My gaze lands on the metal bleachers that house the student section and for a second, it's like I can see a bunch of rowdy high schoolers watching their school team play football. I close my eyes and I see me sitting beside Samantha, bored out of our minds. Then I see Rowen and Kyle and a whole bunch of guys, jumping up and down, yelling and cheering. I feel a smile brush across my face and my eyes snap open as Rowen is pulling my door open.

"Come on, Sade."

I jump down from his truck on my own, making sure my dress lays flat against my legs. We round the back of his truck and I stop dead in my tracks. Up ahead, there's what it looks to be a giant projector, set up just inside the end zone.

"What is that?" I squeal.

Rowen hides his grin as he answers, "It's a movie projector." My mouth gapes open and I look over at him in amazement. This new, older, mature Rowen sure knows how to wow a girl.

I don't have time to say anything because the next thing I know, Rowen's steady hands are around my waist, causing my heart to jump into my throat. He gently places me in the bed of his truck and the moment his hands leave my hips, I suddenly feel let down. *I am in so much trouble with him.*

Once I'm in the truck I realize that there are several blankets and pillows piled in the back, I assume for us to lay on. I'm amazed, simply amazed at the thought he put into this.

As I sit down and crawl over to the back windows, landing softly on the pillows, I say, "This is infinitely better than watching a movie in your parent's basement like we used to..." I laugh as I trail off the last part of the sentence.

One of the first times we ever got somewhat frisky with each other was in his parents old, wood-paneled walled basement while watching some Halloween movie. His parents never really came down to check on us; thank God because they would have seen all sorts of body parts.

"Yeah, well it's been a long three years. My dating skills have gotten infinitely better." He wags his eyebrows up when he crawls up beside me. Then he opens the cracked back window, reaches in and pulls out Twizzlers, and two Diet Cokes. IT JUST KEEPS GETTING BETTER!

"Just wait until you see the movie I picked," he says as he

winks at me. My insides are sizzling. He's not only wowing me with our date but with that damn wink, too.

He clicks something on his phone and then the movie starts up ahead. Once I see what movie is playing, I can't even help the smile breaking out, covering my tiny face.

"Rowen… " I whip my head to his and he has on a small smile, gauging my expression. It's that same Halloween movie from years ago. The first movie we ever watched together. I'm not even sure how he remembers that, I barely do.

He looks so relaxed with his one leg hiked up and his arm draped over it. I don't even have time to think about what I'm doing—I suddenly feel myself quickly move over to him and I throw my arms around his neck. He's stunned, and I am, too, but then he falls into the hug and wraps his other arm around my waist.

Once I let go, I say, "This is the best second first date that I've ever had."

"It's the only second first date you'll ever have." His eyes darken for a second and then we both laugh, turning our attention to the movie. I don't dare move back to my spot. I stay right there, with my body touching Rowen's.

## TWENTY-ONE

Rowen and I's date ended on a perfect note last week. We watched the Halloween movie, sneaking small touches here and there, but by the end of it, we weren't even watching it anymore. We were talking about old memories, his new hopes and dreams, and mine. Our hands were intertwined and I smiled inwardly when I realized that his hand felt so different beneath mine, yet so right. We may be different on the outside, but our hearts are still the same old hearts that never seemed to stop loving.

"Mom, so... " I trail off when I see my dad walking into the kitchen from the back door. I take a deep breath as he stands off to the counter behind my mom, crossing his arms, waiting for me to continue. By the way he is standing, guards up, he knows. He knows Rowen and I are back together. I can feel the tension rolling off his body, just like rain running off a windshield.

"Before you say anything, either of you." I glance in my dad's direction. "Please remember that I'm now twenty-one." My dad snickers and I chuckle. I've literally been twenty-one for like seven hours but whatever. "I'm twenty-one, and I can choose who I want to be with."

No one says anything. My dad rolls his eyes and my mom stands there, waiting patiently for whatever I'm about to say. "With that said, Rowen and I are going out tonight for my birthday." My mom's eyebrows scrunch up in wonder, and I realize it's more than likely because I said the sentence so fast, I sounded like a drunk auctioneer. It came out something like this; "Witsaid, RowIbriday."

"I heard the name Rowen and that's all I need to know." My dad storms past me and it make me feel like crap. I get it, I understand why he's worried. Part of me is, too. I let out an audible huff, blowing my hair off my face, as I turn towards my mom.

"Oh honey, just give him time. I'll talk to him." I must not seem very convinced as she ushers me to sit down and places a huge pile of pancakes in front of me. "Birthday girl's gotta eat!" There's just something about moms that can take your bad mood and make you forget about it, completely. And that's exactly what I do after I take a whiff of the warm, sweet syrup.

ROWEN and I barely work together this summer since he spends most of his days working on the field with the guys, slaying their bodies so they're ready for the football season. I found out on our date that Rowen already has a job set up for after senior year. He'll be the new PE teacher at the high school *and* he'll be assuming the assistant football coach position for a while before climbing the ropes to the athletic director. It's a great plan and I would have never expected anything less from him. He's always been a planner; he's always had his head screwed on straight, except for that whole breaking up with me thing. He lost his mind on that one.

Before going to work, I realize that since I'm going to an undisclosed location with Rowen for my birthday, I'd better make myself presentable and shower in the locker rooms at the club. I don't know why I didn't think about that last time; I guess it was the nerves. I could barely sleep last night, wondering what Rowen had up his sleeves for today. We are definitely taking things slow; he only kissed me on the cheek when we parted a few days ago and we've texted a few times, nothing too clingy or strong. I can't decide if I like that or not. I should like taking things slow, but my libido doesn't. Taking things slow *should* be the route we take, because if go fast, I'll tip over the edge and fall for him quick. Just like three years ago. Our love was one of those fast, fall-for-you-in-a-flash type of loves. The ones that can destroy you in a flash, too.

I told Sash that I'd lock up after showering and he willingly obeyed. I think he's just happy he doesn't have to stay around for stragglers to leave. I shower nice and slow, letting the hot water scald my body. I want to look perfect, and not smell like a swimming pool. It's my twenty-first birthday, so I'm almost positive we'll be going to some type of bar or something along those lines so I planned to wear something sexy but not too dressy.

I blow dry my hair carefully and run my wand through my dark brown locks; giving it a little more wave than usual. I even take the necessary time to put on some more intense make-up, a light smoky-eye and some dark lipstick. When I'm finsihed getting ready, I walk over to the full-length mirror hanging near the door and take a look at myself. I nod my head in approval and grin. That's right, I look HOT. My hair is perfect, my makeup is on point, and the red, strappy summer dress hits just low enough to not show my buttocks. I pair it with some wedges and I walk out the bathroom door, with an evil grin on my face, feeling confident and so unlike the old Sadie. Rowen isn't going to know what to do with me. He's used to teenager Sadie, semi-innocent Sadie. In her place is hot, sexy and grown-up Sadie; with more boob-age, I might add.

Once I lock the iron gate and shut all the lights out, I slowly pace the sidewalk, listening to my wedges pitter patter on the concrete with every step. When I round the corner, I look down and see the the tiniest little pink cupcake sitting there, along with several others. They seem to be leading to something, so I pick up the first, inhaling the sweet-smelling icing, and then walk a few feet forward and pick up the other. There are five in total and once I get to the last one, I bend down to pick it up and my eyes are met with dark shoes. I stand up straight and grin at Rowen. He is leaning against his truck and my mouth waters (not because of the cupcakes, either). He's wearing his dark jeans, and an unbuttoned, light grey button-down with a crisp white shirt underneath. He has paired it with some brown stylish shoes and I'm a little taken back. The old Rowen would have been wearing gym shorts and an old t-shirt with his hat on backwards but this one... this one is freaking edible. Maybe if I place some of this light pink icing on him, I can have a little two in one; it'd be the best present *ever*.

I swallow loudly, as did he. He checks me out from head to toe and his gaze is smoldering. I feel like I'm on fire. *Stop, drop and roll!*

When I look down at his hands, I see he is holding a small box. I slowly walk over to him, still holding the five tiny cupcakes in my hands, and place them on the hood of his truck. We don't say a word, he just hands me the box, untying the silk pink ribbon with his hand. I gulp as I watch his large hand fiddle the ribbon. I suddenly feel like I need to fan myself. When he opens up the box, there lay several pink and white cupcakes in the form of the number 21. I smile and my heart grows soft when I read what was written in manly, scratchy handwriting on the inside flap: Twenty-One cupcakes for my only Cupcake. I think I fall in love with him all over again.

"Happy birthday, Sadie," he says, following a little clear of his throat.

I hastily grab the box out of his hand and put it beside the other cupcakes, and I crowd his space. He looks down at me with confusion lacing his big brown eyes and I tip my head up to his, our lips millimeters from touching. I hear him swallow as I inch closer, placing my timid lips on his. The second our lips touch, I am a goner. Imagine five hundred fireworks going off at the same time. What I mean for the kiss to be, is a sweet way of saying thank you but it turns into something far deeper. It's no longer a sweet and timid kiss. My lips part seconds after they touch his, and his tongue sweeps inside, sweeping me up in the process. I run my fingers through his soft hair and let out an audible moan and he very eagerly does too.

His hands grip my hips, hard, and he whips my body around so it's flat against his truck. His leg goes in between mine, our lips never leaving each other's. This isn't just a kiss shared by two people; this is a "give it back to me kiss," it's a kiss that feels like we will literally fall apart and die if let go.

Needing oxygen, he finally let my lips go and we both gulp up the air like we have been underwater for minutes. I reach up and touch my lips with my fingertips, feeling the swollenness of them, and my mouth turns upwards.

"That was worth waiting for," he says and I reach up and kiss him again, softly this time. If we kiss like that again, we won't make it to wherever we are going. I can promise you that.

Rowen backs away once I remove my lips and runs his hand over his face, calming himself down. I get it, I need a breather too. Once he looks back at me, he gives me that Rowen grin and says, "You look absolutely beautiful, Sadie." I flush in response and grab my cupcakes, rounding the front of his truck, smiling the entire time.

Once we get closer to where we're going, Rowen makes me tie a blindfold around my face. I scowl the entire time I am tying it behind my head but really, I'm euphoric over the idea of being surprised.

When I feel the rumble of his truck come to a stop I try to look through the blindfold to see where exactly we are. I can't make out shit, so I sit here and cross my arms—pouting like a four-year-old.

"This is a bit ridiculous, Rowen." I roll my eyes underneath the blindfold.

"Relax, Sade. We're here." I huff in response but feel him shift closer to me.

"Do you remember what you said we'd do on your twenty-first birthday?" he whispers along my ear, causing goosebumps to break out all over my arms.

"No, I don't think so... " I try to think really hard but with his breath on my neck, I just can't concentrate.

"We were at Kyle's. In his bedroom. You, me, Kyle, and I think it was... "

I finish the sentence for him, "Katelyn." Kyle's flavor of the month. He went through more girls than I could count on my fingers... and my toes.

"Mmhm," his breath warm on my neck. "And we were all drunk, playing quarters and you looked right at me and said... " He trails off and lets me finish.

"I looked over at you, after making my quarter in the cup, and I said, 'You're gonna take me to all the bars along College Street and get drunk with me. Then you're going to carry me back home.'" I laugh when I say it. I was tipsy at the time, without a care in the world.

I feel Rowen's hand brush my cheek as he unties the blindfold from my face and sure enough, here we are, parked in front of College Street. This is where all the bars are, all the good ones, anyway. The ones you come to on your twenty-first birthday planning to get shit-faced.

I've been to bars before, the ones near Duke, but never as a twenty-one year old, and these establishments are so different in all aspects. The street is lined with cars, people spilling out of the buildings plastered beside one another. They are all brick, and rusty looking. Young women, clad in tight dresses, and high heels, and curled hair. Men dressed to impress, trying to catch a whiff of any female that walked past. Carefree, fun.

"This is the best second second date I've ever had," I laugh as Rowen climbs out of his truck.

He turns around at the last second, "And it's the last second second date you'll ever have." I bloom on the inside. Literally bloom like a flower on a spring day.

Once we enter the first bar, we are taken back to a back booth and there are Anna, Hannah Marie, Kyle and some other guy. I almost jumped for joy at the sight of my friends but Rowen's hand landed on my lower back and my spine straightened right up. His touch does things to me, especially after our hasty make-out session. I still feel his hands on my body, his lips on mine. I'm probably still flushed, too.

"Happy birthday!" Anna and Hannah say in unison, draping a hot pink feather boa over my shoulders and placing a sparkly "Birthday Girl" crown on top of my head. Kyle already had a birthday drink in hand for me and I downed it in seconds. I needed a drink to calm my raging hormones. With Rowen's touch on me, claiming me in this busy upbeat bar, I'm ready to strip down naked.

We all ended up taking a few shots (except the mystery guy, who I find out later is a friend from school that they paid to be the DD), and then we wobbled around to three more bars. We were currently in Crazy Eight's and it was by far my favorite. It was big and open. A giant dancefloor right smack dab in the middle. The place was decked out in neon every-thing. Everything glowed like we were in a laser tag maze and the dim lights made everyone look as if we were avatars.

"Shots for the birthday girl!" Hannah slurs and I willingly take the shot, tipping my head back and letting the burning liquid slide down my throat. I had a pretty good tolerance, thanks to Alicia and I hitting several parties last year (in hopes to get my mind off Rowen, which obviously didn't work) but now that I'm at my fourth bar, I'm drunk. Straight up drunk and you know how I know that? Because I just dragged Hannah Marie and Anna out onto the dance floor with me. I'm in between the duo, with my hands in the air, letting my hair whip across my face.

Hannah Marie and Anna are basically grinding on me and we're all cracking up like we're in a comedy show. I glance over at Rowen and he's sitting at the bar, a beer in his oversized hand, cracking a smile at me with the pink feather boa wrapped around his shoulders.

My heart grows about ten times its size and I can't take it any longer. I slip out from in between the girls and I push and shove my way towards my man. I keep walking past him, giving him a wink (a definite effect of being inebriated) and step outside the side door.

The sun has completely set now, the moon barely peeking

out from behind a dark grey cloud. Seconds later, I hear the door swing open with its creaky hinges and Rowen is walking out. The music and chattering pours through the open door and then it's slammed shut again, leaving only Rowen and I in the dark alley. He has lost the pink feather boa and his hair looks effortlessly tousled. He looks down at me, shadows covering his dark eyes, and cocks an eyebrow. I grab his hand and pull him close to me, smacking my lips onto his. I taste the hint of a dark beer on his tongue and listen to him growl under my touch. Our hands are everywhere. His on my lower back, reaching around to cup my head. Mine on his biceps, squeezing and scratching for more. I need more. He's like a drug that I'll never stop needing. He quickly spins us around and backs me up against the side of the bar. I can feel the warm brick along my exposed shoulder blades and Rowen lifts my hands so they're pinned above my head. He dips down and kisses my neck.

"Jesus, Sadie. I can't—" he kisses me along my collar bone and I realize that I'm gasping like a wild animal but I don't care. I want *more.*

His lips hit mine again and they're just as eager as before. Nipping my lips with his teeth, I let out a breathy moan. I hurriedly buck my hips up to his and I can feel his hardness from outside his jeans. Excited, I give his lip a little bite which just seems to make things that much hotter. This is probably the most amazing sexual experience I have ever had. It's rushed, and raw; no time for second guessing, no time to slow down. He puts me into a completely different state of ecstasy. It's as if all our past is catching up to us, emotion after emotion pouring from our very veins. It's fierce, and breathtaking.

I breathe his name, "Rowen." He hums against my ear as he rubs himself against me. This is different. What we have now, it's different; it's down-right emotional and sexy.

He growls and I feel it rumble against my chest. He backs up fast and his face is flushed. I pout when he steps away and he shakes his head at me.

"We have to stop."

I whine and I'm surprised at how bratty I'm being. "Why?"

"Because you're drunk," he says, as a matter-of-fact.

"No, I'm not!" And he laughs and then I laugh because I slurred my words. Even my drunken ears can realize that.

"Come here," I say and he willingly does. I press my lips against his again and he laughs against them.

"Sadie. Stop tempting me... " he kisses me hard again and then takes a step back and pauses. When he leans in again, it's only to give me a quick peck on the lips. Then he grabs my hand, breaking the tethered rope we just had tying us together. "Just imagine how fucking good it'll be when we're both sober." I pause. I think. And then I break out into a devious smile, following him back into the bar.

## TWENTY-TWO

It's been two weeks since Rowen and I have started up again and I can't say that my mind and heart are on talking terms. It's like my heart is lapping up the feeling Rowen gives me just as a dog laps up water after a hot day in the sun. Then my mind, she's cowering in the back of the classroom like a student who doesn't want to be picked by the teacher. The rational part of my mind is scared to death that Rowen is going to leave me again, because I don't know if I'll be able to pick myself up. This time with us is so unlike the last time. It's much more powerful than our little high school love.

We've had several more dates together. Nothing as elaborate as the first date, per se but each one still makes my heart flutter. Sometimes we just talk after work, hanging out on the bed of his truck in the parking lot of the club, stealing simple touches and hot and heavy make-out sessions, and a few times we probably could have gotten charged with indecent exposure crimes. But we still haven't had sex, which is a huge step to take. I want to speed things up but at the same time, the more I get intimate with him, the more I fall for him—so here I am, teetering over the edge of the Grand Canyon. Trying to grab onto the rusty copper boulders like they're a lifeline.

The entire town knows about us now. It was only a matter of time before the old ladies that cluster together at Joe's coffee patio every morning knew. They're the pot-stirrers of this town: gossiping about the latest fling between couples, who stole the town flag, that kind of stuff. Crazy old bats, if you ask me. They started on us the second we took the final step and went out in public, holding hands. Yes, holding hands—big whoop, huh? Well, according to Mrs. Silinsky it was a big freaking deal. Even my parents mentioned it.

"I see you and Rowen are taking the next step... " my dad had grumbled under his coffee. I couldn't help but roll my eyes.

"Oh, stop it hun. They're in their twenties, they're adults. Let them make their own decisions." My mom winked at me from a distance and I mouthed a simple "thank you."

Of course, Rowen's parents are fine with the pair of us starting up again. His parents always liked me, and hey, I didn't go around stomping all over Rowen's heart. We still don't feel the need to hang out at one of our houses. I told him it made me feel like I was in high school again, and he agreed. Although, I know he's just happy with not having to see my dad.

"Hey, Sadie. I'm gonna go. Can you lock up after the Kerry's leave?" I bluntly roll my eyes at the Kerry's sloowwwy packing up their gear. They are, by far, the slowest freaking people on the planet. I half think they do it on purpose. They like seeing "the help" have to wait around for them. Mrs. Kerry comes to the pool every single day, and every single day, she is decked out in some different, sparkly diamond necklace, an enormous black sunhat and a skimpy one-piece bathing suit. (You know, the kind that forms a V in between her breasts to her belly button). She waves her children off and goes on to reading her magazine, all while sipping leisurely on a margarita. She's high-class, that's for sure.

"Yeah, sure. I'll lock up." I don't bother telling Sash I'm using the showers to get ready again. I don't think we're really supposed to use these showers to actually shower with shampoo and all that good-smelling stuff. They're built to wash off the chlorine and that's it, but I can't very well go into the clubhouse and use those showers. I'm not a member, remember?

When the Kerry's finally get their things and leave, I go over and clean up the rest of their mess. Dispose of the sticky ice cream wrappers, take the empty margarita glass to the concessions area, and wipe down their table. Then I hear a voice.

"I like that angle," Rowen quips, raising an eyebrow, and I give him a death stare. Except really, I'm blooming on the inside. Maybe these bathing suits aren't so bad after all.

"Are you ready?" he says, as he walks up from behind me, taking the rag and finishing cleaning the table.

"No, not even close. I need to shower. Will you keep watch?" He leans around me, wrapping his bare hands on my wet suit. The butterflies flutter all over my skin. No matter how many times he leans in to kiss me, I still get all flushed and nervous.

"Of course." He pecks me on the cheek and follows me to the shower, leaning against the outside entrance as I grab my things. I walk barefoot on the white and blue tile floor; it's a pretty extravagant locker room with its crystal white tiled walls and light blue accents, especially considering it's only for washing the pool grime off your body.

I almost feel a little scandalous shimmying out my bathing suit while Rowen is a simple ten feet from me, propped up against the door. He's there and here I am, naked and basically wanting to invite him in to join me. I shake my head and tell myself it's too soon, even though my hormones are saying something different. I step into the scalding hot shower and take a deep breath, letting the water cascade down my body, relieving my pent-up nerves. Once I go to reach for my shampoo, I mouth, "Shit." I forgot it in my bag and I definitely need it or else this shower will be pointless. My hair will still smell like chlorine, and I don't want to smell like chlorine. I want to look and smell as good as Rowen does, all washed and devourable.

"Rowen?" I yell out, while peeking my head away from the water running into my mouth.

"Yeah? You okay?" he yells back.

"I'm fine, but I forgot my shampoo in my bag; can you grab it and bring it? The bag is by the door." Before he can step in here, I also yell, "But close your eyes when you come in here. There aren't curtains." These are not private showers, like I said; they're only here to wash off the chlorine.

I hear him chuckle. It's nothing he hasn't seen before, but we're on a different playing field now. My breasts are fuller than when I was that tiny seventeen-year-old girl. I have more curves, and I look like a woman. I'm not ready for him to see me yet. I want to be ready, I want to be in sexy lingerie; I want it to be planned... I think.

"Okay, I'm coming in."

When I see him walking into the locker room, holding my strawberry shampoo in one hand, I let out a little laugh. He has his other hand slapped across his face, covering his eyes. He walks in the direction of the sound of the water and I say, "A few steps to the right," hiding my snicker. His foot hits the wall and he grunts.

"Stop messing with me or I'll uncover my eyes." I roll my

eyes and glower at the tiny voice in the back of my head saying, "Do it."

He walks a few more feet towards me and says, "It's taking every bit of willpower that I have to keep my eyes shut… " My heart starts beating even faster in my chest as I take the bottle from his hand, our fingers just barely skimming. He turns back around, facing the direction of the door, and un-prys his hand from his face. He walks a few feet as I pour my pink shampoo in my hand, letting the air fill with the smell of sweet strawberries. I rub the shampoo through my hair and stare at his back, feeling the intense desire between the two of us.

"That smells the exact same as it did three years ago. Sweet… " His voice is hoarse and his back is rigid. I don't say anything as I wash the shampoo out of my hair.

The time it takes me to wash my hair seems excruciatingly long. He doesn't move the entire time and then I suddenly feel bold. "Rowen… " He turns around in a flash and walks over to me, grabbing my slippery torso and putting his forehead to mine, barely glancing down at my exposed body. The water is pouring over the two of us and he inhales sharply, taking in my strawberry shampoo.

"You know, every time I smelled any type of strawberry scent, I wanted to bang my fist against a wall. Even the mere glimpse of a strawberry would drive me insane. I couldn't keep the memories away, no matter how fucking hard I tried. Every single thing reminded me of you. Everything."

I stayed silent, only nodding my head against his, because it was the same for me. Everything reminded me of him or of some type of memory. The boy in my Public Speaking class that would shake his hair out of habit… Rowen. The smell of freshly cut grass… Rowen. A deep, musky scent… Rowen. Everything screamed Rowen.

Rowen's hands trail up my bare back and I arch out of reaction, feeling his wet shirt on my breasts. How badly, I wish that he were bare-chested like me. I step up on my tiptoes and place my mouth on his, sensually and full of passion. My chest rises and falls with every stroke of his tongue. He dips his mouth down to my neck; I move it slightly to the right to allow more access. I can feel myself melting beneath his touch. I feel myself coming undone, just with his lips on my slick body. Maybe it's the water, maybe it's something in the air, but I can feel myself trembling.

I reach my hands under his shirt and pull the wet, heavy material away from his body. I run my fingers down his abs as his trail down past my belly button. I follow his cue and just as I'm reaching my hand into his shorts, I hear a woman's laugh coming from near the door. My head snaps that direction and Rowen quickly spurs into action. He turns the water off, throws my towel at me, and gathers my bag, all while dragging me into the far bathroom stall. I wanted to laugh so hard. (It was one of those moments where you know you shouldn't laugh and you should actually be quite nervous but the bubbling laugh inside of you desperately wants to come out—that was me, in this moment.) I snicker, unable to hold it together, and Rowen looks like he is going to bust at the seams, smashing his lips together and clenching his eyes. He covers my mouth and shakes his head "no" at me. I suddenly stop laughing, as I can still feel my desire to undress him the rest of the way, even in this tiny bathroom stall. We'd been interrupted and as much as I should be afraid that we are gonna get caught, I just want to do it all over again. When Rowen's eyes meet mine for the second time, I can still see the desire swirling in them. I lick my lips, almost reaching up to get a taste, again.

"Are you sure no one will come in here?" a woman says. I

can tell she's an older woman; her voice is one laced with sophistication. It's a woman whose heels are clicking on the wet tile.

"I promise." I hear Sash's voice and I meet Rowen's wide-eyed expression. I know my my face has to mimic his, as I feel my own eyes grow large.

"You promise what... ?" The women's voice is dripping with sex and I cannot believe what I am hearing.

"I promise, Mrs. Richards... ma'am." My mouth opens up and I swear I could swallow the entire world. Rowen puts his finger to my lips, shushing me.

This woman, is the club owner's wife. The wife of a man who is probably the richest person in this entire city, hell, maybe even this entire state. They have four kids, who are all teenagers—meaning that Mrs. Richards is definitely in her forties. Holy crap! Sash is having an affair with the club owner's wife, and you know how I know that? Because I can hear the smacking of lips and audible moans coming from her mouth.

"Why is it wet in here?" she says, out of breath. I put my hand over my mouth, to keep myself from gasping out loud.

"I guess someone showered before leaving."

"Ugh, disgusting. Let's go somewhere dry. I don't want my hair ruined." I roll my eyes and almost snicker, but Rowen's rough hand covers my mouth and he has on a small smile, holding in his laugh.

"Come on, hottie." she says, and I shut my eyes so hard to keep myself from hearing anything else, although that doesn't work because I hear with my ears, not my eyes. The second I hear her giggles become distant, Rowen's hand leaves my mouth and I literally lose it. I crack up so hard that my stomach cramps.

"Oh my God!" I say, through another fit of laughter. I grip

the towel I have around my body, just so it doesn't fall off with my incessant cackling.

Rowen shakes his wet hair, spraying my face and says, "What a fucking night." I meet his stare and we crack up a little bit longer, all while sneaking out of the bathroom stall. I throw my clothes on fast, watching Rowen's gaze linger over my most intimate parts. I know that look, I remember him drinking me up when we were younger, although this look is filled with much more desire. The desire of a man. I'm thankful that Sash flipped the lights off; that way Rowen can't see just how much he affects me.

"CAMPING?" I exclaim. "But Alicia is coming down for your party!"

Rowen, Kyle, and I are hanging out at the football stadium, our old hangout spot (minus Samantha). We all used to sneak out here, climb the metal football stands, sit up at the very top, overlooking the town's lights flashing and drink whatever kind of beer we'd brought. Normally it would be the cheapest thing we could get their hands on. I didn't usually drink, which led them to calling me, Goody Two-Shoes. Everyone but Rowen called me that. He'd snarl in their direction and tell them I didn't have to drink if I didn't want to. But tonight, I'm totally drinking. After all, it's legal now.

"Relax, it's still a party. It's just out at my parents' lake house." Kyle retaliates.

"Oh, okay then. Good." Alicia is coming tomorrow night and I guess instead of going to Kyle's fancy rich house, we're going to the lake instead. I quickly grab my phone and tell her to bring a bathing suit and bug spray and she sends me back a thumbs up emoticon followed by another emoticon that shows a girl with her hands up in confusion.

"So, tell me more about this Alicia." Kyle intones while Rowen grabs my tiny waist, snuggling my body in between his.

"Alicia is amazing. She's kind-hearted but also a little wild. She's never on time, for anything... " Rowen laughs and responds, "Which probably drives you crazy." I purse my lips, but he's right.

Kyle chuckles, "Okay, but what does she look like? Show me a picture." I grab my phone and scroll through the million pictures I have of Alicia and I, stopping at a snapshot of us from one of the football games. I pick this one because it shows just how beautiful she is. Sure, I could have shown him the one from Halloween when she was dressed like a slutty nurse, but in this one, she looks beautiful. Her dark-olive skin is glowing under the stadium lights and she's laughing at something I said. Her bright jade eyes are shining against the dark contrast of her skin and hair. She has that perfect hair. The kind every single girl wishes she had; shiny and perfectly wavy. I used to get so envious when she'd wake up, fluff her fingers through her hair and look just as good as the night before.

I don't even remember who took the picture as I stare at it longer. I'm in it with her and then I feel my eyes widen a little. It's not just a picture of Alicia and I; Library Boy is in it, too, holding my hand. I look over at Rowen and watch as his gaze zeros in on the hand-holding. I feel his knees shift a little and he instantly goes stiff. Kyle mumbles something like, "Hot damn, she's attractive," but he also feels the shift in the air. All of a sudden, I feel like I'm in trouble. Like Rowen has just caught me doing the neighbor or something. But, that can't be right because he and I were nothing last year. I was simply trying to find myself (read as: trying to get Rowen *out* of my system).

"And I'm out... " Kyle jumps up, glancing between the pair of us. "See you two tomorrow."

With Kyle out of ear distance, I take in Rowen's posture. He's definitely mad, or upset. His jaw is clenched tight, muscles playing at the sides of his face. His fists are balled together and if I look closely enough, I can see his chest rising and falling quicker than normal beneath his blue shirt.

"So, that's what you were doing all year?" I close the picture on the phone, hearing it click, and I blink a few times, trying to figure out what to say.

"Did you expect me not to see anyone else in the last three years that we've been apart?" My voice comes out ragged, full of emotion.

"I don't know what I expected."

"You can't honestly tell me that you haven't seen another girl since everything... " As much as it pains me to say it, I know it's true. He's been with other girls. I know he has, otherwise he wouldn't be have been so damn confident during our little sexual session in the shower the other night.

"I've seen other girls, Sadie." My heart plummets. Ouch. "But none of them came even close to you."

I blurt, "And none of the guys came close to you... why do you think I came back to the club this year? I tried to date, I even had sex to try to rid you from my brain and guess what. It didn't work."

His head whips to mine and I realize that I just told him I had sex with someone else. I feel like I've stepped over the imaginary line we drew for one another last year. My face instantly feels hot.

"You had sex?" He accentuates the word "sex" and my

face gets even hotter. Just slap on some bacon and it'll be sizzling in no time.

"Haven't you?" His expression says it all. He looks away from me quickly, trying to hide the guilt.

We don't speak for a few minutes and I can't decide what to say. I almost feel the guilt eating me alive that I actually had sex with someone I didn't love, all to get rid of someone I did love.

"I'm sorry." I whisper and he quickly grabs my waist and pulls taut around his knees.

"You shouldn't be sorry. I led us to this." That little devil on my shoulder is nodding her head. I scowl inwardly. "Plus, I wasn't exactly a monk during the last three years."

"So, you've been with a lot of other girls?" I feel my heart cracking. Snap, crackle and pop. That's my heart right now.

"I had sex a lot that first year of school. I was trying to just stop thinking about you. The attack, leaving you, this... " He reaches up and softly touches my now faded scar. "It didn't work. It just made me crave you that much more." I see the desire swarming in the air. Despite the conversation we're having; I still just want him to pick me up and lay me flat on one of these bleacher benches and show me just how much he regrets the last three years.

I whisper as softly as the wind is blowing, "I feel like the last three years have just been us going around in circles, destroying each other. Over and over again."

His thumb moves over my lower lip and he runs the pad of his finger over it. "Then let's just stop." I give him a weak smile and move onto his lap. He kisses my bare shoulder and we stare out onto the field for a long time, lost in the thousands of memories whirling around us.

## TWENTY-THREE

Alicia is literally bouncing off the walls. She's getting to "party with my high school gang", and she hasn't shut up about meeting Rowen. I've filled her in on just about everything, leaving out the whole Sash/affair part. She keeps mumbling on about how my life is more exciting than a soap opera. I roll my eyes and nudge her out the door when Kyle's black Land Rover pulls up.

He yells, "Let's go, Sadie!", and I can hear him all the way from inside. I laugh as Alicia and I both head out the front door, waving to my dad (who is scowling in the corner) and mom. My dad didn't believe that we were going camping until he watched us descend down the stairs from my bedroom. Alicia and I thought it would be hilarious to look the part of campers so we're both wearing cut-off shorts, plain tanks and flannel shirts wrapped around our waists, all paired with hiking boots. We actually look cute, for a pair of campers, that is.

When we run outside, Rowen and Kyle both step out of the Rover to grab our bags and I briefly introduce Kyle and Alicia. Kyle reaches in and hugs her and her eyes shoot open and she mouths "OH MY GOD!" from behind his back. I giggle and Rowen shakes his head. Kyle is extremely attractive in a boyish kind of way: from the way his blonde hair (even blonder now from the summer sun) peeks out from his baseball cap, to his dimpled smile, Kyle makes all the girls salivate at the mouth.

"Rowen?" I hear my dad's voice from the front door and freeze. Oh, crap! Rowen looks at me and takes a deep breath while briefly shaking his head as he makes his way to the front porch, which inevitably is where my dad is standing with his arms crossed like some type of military instructor. It's quite funny to see my dad act tough. He's short and on the smaller side in general, to be honest, he isn't the least bit intimidating.

I watch from outside the car as he and my dad talk. My dad looks to be saying a lot to him. This is vastly different from the first time they met. Rowen was such a young boy, still on the larger side with his long legs, but not as macho as he is now. Now, it's two men talking, man to man. I see Rowen reach his hand out in an attempt to shake my dad's, and I still my breathing. My dad looks down at his hand and then back at Rowen's face and finally gives in. He shakes it and then swiftly lets go, walking back in the house. Rowen is wearing a smug smile as he reaches for the car door and ushers me inside. For a moment there, I felt like I was watching Animal Planet; Will the lion pounce on its prey, or will they come to terms?

"What was that about?" I pipe up as soon as we take off down the road.

Kyle glances back. "Yeah, I was half-expecting to I was going to have to peel him off of you. I for sure thought he would kick your ass." I hear Alicia snicker from the front seat.

"Oh, he just wanted to know what my intentions were with his daughter."

"And... ?" I question.

"And I told him my intentions were to marry you." If I were drinking something, it would be splayed all over the back of Kyle's headrest. My eyes almost fall out of my head. Alicia turns around to take in my expression and busts up laughing. I give her my evil eyes, narrowing them into slits, which on me doesn't really look mean at all. A laugh erupts from everyone. I cross my arms and look out the window, ignoring all three of them.

North Carolina is known for its beauty of beaches and perfect weather but what we natives know, is that North Carolina has various hidden spots, the ones that are so extraordinarily beautiful that you think you've died and gone to heaven. And this hidden lake is just that... heaven.

As we pull up to Kyle's parents' lake house, I am amazed at its size. It's enormous with its numerous white stairs coiling up to the front door. It's built up on high white pillars which I assume is because this so-called lake is more like a small inlet off the ocean. The house sits up high, overlooking the small, makeshift beach down below, which leads out onto a small pier, all on top of the salty water. This place is the best of both worlds, beachy *and* woodsy, with tall trees surrounding us. The air even smells salty like the ocean but also with a touch of forest.

"This is beautiful, Kyle," I whisper as I step further out of the car. I look up and see the sun casting its pretty glow through the openings of the green limbs.

"Wow, I have been missing out all my life... " Alicia grabs my hand and we run over to the edge of the grass and look down at the little beach. Off to the side lays a rustic-looking wooden ladder, so we pull it up and shove it down below us, climbing down so fast that the guys have to search for us.

"I can't believe you didn't tell me how freaking hot Kyle is;

you totally held back." I glance over at Alicia and give her a little shrug. Kyle is hot, but he's nothing compared to my Rowen. My Rowen? Oh my God.

"Sorry, I forgot. You only have eyes for Rowen." She emphasizes his name and I half roll my eyes. But she's right, I do only have eyes for him and that's the dangerous part. "I can see why, though."

"Whatever," I joke.

"Enough boy-talk. Let's go get drinks and start this day." I follow her up the ladder and silently yell at my conscience catching up to me, telling me to run before Rowen can destroy me all together.

THE ENTIRE DAY has been exhausting, but I'm so liberated that I don't even realize how tired I am. My limbs ache and I'm a bit tipsy, but I can't seem to care. We've been out on Kyle's boat for most of the afternoon, jet skiing and tubing, and we even got to see a few dolphins. There's jellyfish and dolphins that inhabit this small bayou, especially in the summer. Kyle kept warning us to stay clear of the jellyfish and he complained how he's been stung more times than he could count, but they didn't bother me. I told him I'm never leaving.

Once it started to hit dusk, the sky burning with pinks and oranges, Alicia and I had the notion to feed the guys then others started to show up, Hannah Marie and Anna being two of them, lugging a giant cooler full of something called "Jungle Juice." Rowen muttered under his breath that they call it "Death Juice" at UNC because it'll knock you on your ass faster than you can even say "ouch." It looked tasty and smelled of oranges and some type of fruit punch; in fact, there was even some fruit floating around in its reddish tint.

The rest of the people who showed up I wasn't really familiar with. A couple of them were from UNC, and a few from neighboring schools. The few girls that did come seemed nice at first, but they'd make small talk with Rowen and my blood would boil. I made sure each of them watched as I claimed him. I would grab his hand and kiss him on the cheek, sending off an aura of "DO NOT TOUCH" around us. Rowen did the same; he would snake his arms around my waist, placing playful kissed along my collarbone. It was frankly hilarious at how we were claiming each other and I was really unaware until Alicia mentioned it.

"You two are going to start peeing on each other soon," she cracks and I whip my head at her so fast I almost drop my drink on the ground.

"What?" I exclaim.

"You and Rowen are making it perfectly clear that you are each other's and no one else's." Rowen chuckles behind me and Alicia smashes her lips together to keep herself from laughing. Kyle pipes in with his laughter, too. My face heats as I think for a moment. I decide that she's right, but I also decide that I don't care. So, I do what any sane girl would do. I reach my arms around Rowen's neck and kiss him passionately. I'm aware that we have an audience; I just don't care.

Rowen nips my lip and I almost moan. Instead, I sit up quickly, placing my jungle juice on the chair, and grab his hand. He trails behind me and we can both hear people hooting and hollering but we just keep on trekking. Once I let go of his hand to climb down the ladder, I bask in the scratchy wooden rods along my hands. Rowen follows me down, just as I land in the soft, warm sand, and asks what I'm doing. I only grin at him, stumbling a little as I climb up the small makeshift wooden pier and walk to the very edge. With Rowen right behind me, I turn around and reach up on my tiptoes and kiss him gently on the lips, just enough to he can have a taste of the juice on my mouth and then I back away, toying with the hem of my shirt.

"What are you doing?" he inquires, watching my fingers trail down to the bottom of my shirt.

"We're goin' swimmin'." I lift my shirt up over my head and drop it to my feet. I'm left standing there in my jean shorts and lacy, pale-pink bra. The only light around us is from the moon and it casts a perfect glow on our bodies, our reflections shining brightly on the ripples of the salt water.

Rowen looks back up to where the party is, bites his lip unintentionally, and then his gaze saunters back over to me.

"Oh, stop it. Who cares if they see us." I wink and I watch his Adam's apple bobble up and down.

"I don't want anyone else to see you like this." He takes the few steps left between us to get to my body and wraps his warm hand around my torso. He tilts my head up to his, and I'm staring into his long-lashed eyes when he swiftly leans down to kiss me, hard. His tongue swirls with mine and my hand moves to grip his unruly hair. He stops the kiss abruptly and whispers, "I want to be the only man on this earth to watch you strip your clothes down to your bra and panties." I chuckle and push his chest lightly so I can continue on my journey. Even in the moonlight, I can see his eyes darken when my fingers reach the button on my shorts. I slowly unbutton them, hearing the zipper click among the sound of small waves crashing, and then they drop, just like that.

"So, you're saying no to skinny-dipping?" I intone, standing there, almost completely naked.

"I'm not saying no, but if you strip down naked right here in front of me I cannot promise that I will keep my hands to myself." I think for a moment, debating. We agreed to take things slow, but the sex kitten inside of me is slowly losing her ability to reason.

"You can touch me... " I say coyly. "But, no sex. Not tonight."

He takes a deep breath and nods as his gazes follows my bare legs, "Whatever you want, babe."

I saunter over to him and lift his shirt up over his head just as he unbuttons his pants. I teasingly run my hand over his most intimate part and he grunts in response, digging his hands roughly onto my hips.

He quickly nips my ear and I can feel my lower parts heat with fire. I back us to the edge of the pier and just as my eyes meet his, a smile breaks out on my face. He looks perplexed, raising one eyebrow, and I quickly step back and shove him into the water, alone.

I hear a splash and look down as he emerges from the water. I'm cracking up, holding my middle and he has on his award-winning Rowen smile, bright teeth shining against the backdrop of the bayou.

"You little brat!" he yells, and I laugh harder. "I'm coming up there to get you."

I squeal when his wet hand grips my foot and pulls me into the warm salty water with him. By the end, we're both in the water laughing so hard that people start yelling at us from above. I wrap my bare legs around his torso, noticing that I feel at home, even in this giant pool of water.

His lips capture mine again but this time it's slower, more meaningful. Every time we kiss, it's like we're starved for one another. Every time he runs his hands over my body, it's because he forgets what I feel like. Things are so rushed lately, until this moment. He caresses my lips with his, moving his tongue languidly with mine. I reach up and run my fingers through his wet locks, and feel my heart emerge from its hiding spot. I lean back, breaking our intimate kiss, and look him dead in the eye. In that exact moment, Rowen looks directly into my soul and I into his; in that moment, our souls reconnect and I know that we're back in the race. I just wonder where the finish line is.

BY THE TIME we make our way back up to the party, it's died down. Some people are still sitting by the fire, but it's mostly quiet. Everyone is more than likely passing out from their day-drinking. Alicia is staying with Kyle, which she made very clear to every male and female attending this party, and something I know that Kyle is more than pleased with. When I unzip the zipper to Rowen's and my tiny tent (yes, even though there is a perfectly fine lake house only a few yards away, we're staying in tents), I see that Rowen has laid out two sleeping bags. He climbs in the tent with me, looks at the two sleeping bags, back at me, and then back to the bags again.

"I wasn't sure what you wanted so I just grabbed two." I shake my head and crawl over to the maroon sleeping bag, unzipping it all the way. Then I crawl over to the other black sleeping bag and lay it on top of the first; spreading them both out, using one as a blanket and one as a pallet.

"I need someone to keep me warm." I give him a tiny smile and he relaxes.

"Thank God," he mumbles.

I quickly change out of my wet garments while Rowen is inside the house grabbing us some waters and when he comes back, I'm already lying under the sleeping bags. He zips it up and climbs in beside me. I scoot right over to his warm body and nuzzle my head onto his chest, breathing in the salty residue from our swim. I can tell my senses are in overdrive because I just keep smelling him and cuddling up to his warm body like I can't get enough. I have to shush the rational part of my brain that keeps telling me to be careful, to keep my guard up. Instead I listen to the other half—the half that is relishing Rowen's scent. This is what I want. I want to lay on his chest, and listen to the familiarity of his heartbeat as I fall asleep, forever.

## TWENTY-FOUR

I go back to school in less than a month. I have no idea how the summer went by this fast, but it did. It doesn't feel fair. Normally I'm wishing that summer would fly by so I could get away from Rowen, but here I am, almost distraught that I'm about to go back to school without him. I know we don't have to draw that invisible line this summer like the rest. When we both go back to school, not much about our relationship will change. We're less than an hour away from each other, so I shouldn't be feeling like the end is nearing but I am and I can't quite shake it. The second I'm away from Rowen I can't stop the dooming thoughts of what might happen. What if he leaves me again? What if he just cuts me out of his life like he did before? It literally keeps me up at night, tossing and turning, but when I'm with him, the worried voice is silent. Gone. The thoughts go away, the fighting hold I have with ignoring them disappears. It's like he washes away all the bad in the world. He washes away all the worry.

We've taken things slow this summer, just getting to know one another again. We still haven't had sex yet and I'm happy with that because I know the moment we do, I'll be hooked.

I'll be hooked so deeply onto him that I don't think I'll be able to untangle myself if need be. I have to say that I'm proud of how Rowen has been able to keep from taking me hostage and having his way with me; Lord knows I've teased him enough.

Just as I turn over in bed, I see my phone light up. I grab it, and force away the smile that slithers onto my face. Rowen's name has popped up and I feel like it's Christmas morning.

**Rowen:** Open your window.

I sit up quickly in bed and text him back.

**Me:** Why?
**Rowen:** Because I'm climbing up.
**Me:** Rowen, we're not teenagers anymore. You don't have to sneak through my window like before.
**Rowen:** I don't care how old we are. Your dad is never going to be okay with me sneaking in your house at one in the morning.

I let out a small laugh and stand up to adjust my large night shirt. I pad over to my window, hearing it unfasten, and sure enough I see Rowen's strong body swinging himself up on the giant oak tree. I shake my head at his barely visible body. He grins and I step away from my window, giving him room to barely squeeze his large frame through my window.

When he stands up and brushes the leaves from his jacket, he looks back at my window. I look around to see what he's staring at and he says, "Did you guys get smaller windows?"

I stifle a laugh. "No, you're just a lot bulkier than you were at seventeen," I whisper.

He wags his eyebrows and quietly slides my window down. I can't help but watch his back as he closes it. I can already feel the tug in my middle.

"What are you doing here?" I ask, as I gather my hair to one side.

"What I should have done a long time ago." My eyebrows scrunch together as he stalks toward me. He grabs my face in his hands and smashes his lips onto mine. It doesn't take me more than a second to oblige as I force my tongue inside his mouth. His hands are under my shirt in seconds, and the feel of his bare skin on mine heats my entire body. He lifts my shirt up over my head and I'm left standing in my darkened childhood bedroom, with nothing on but my silk lilac panties. I don't give him time to stare as I'm kissing him feverishly again. I feel possessed as I rip his jacket and shirt off. He lifts me up and my legs willingly wrap themselves around his tight torso. He walks us over to my unmade full-sized bed and lays me flat against the sheets. He gathers my hands and raises them above my head, trailing kisses all the way from the crook of my neck to the very bottom of my belly button. I'm squirming so fervently that he has to pause to make sure I'm okay.

This is so different than when we were kids. When we were kids, we had nervous, trembling hands. We had no idea what we were doing—only taking each other to learn about the opposite sex's anatomy. Back then, it was like he had a roadmap to my body, except it only had dead end streets and flickering stoplights. Now... now he has the perfect navigational system leading him right to where I need him to be.

He has one hand holding mine above my head and the other is slowly trailing down to my panties. His lips are distracting me as they, too, follow his hands, leaving small kisses everywhere he touches. I can feel myself start to build up, and he hasn't even really starting doing anything. Once his hand reaches my panties, he pulls them aside and not even a second later I feel his warm mouth on my middle. I arch my back instantly and choke out a quiet moan, well aware that my parents are sleeping two rooms away from mine.

Rowen licks and sucks and laps me up until I'm on the verge of coming apart. My toes are starting to curl, my insides turning to lava; he is slowly undoing every single part of me. He finally lets go of my other hand and I'm thankful because I'm eager. I'm eager to feel him inside me; I'm eager to feel that passion from the both of us.

I sit up quickly and start to undo his belt; I'm proud at how fast my fingers move to get his pants off. Once they're thrown on the floor, he's only left in his boxers but I don't waste a single minute. I push my fingers inside and strip him down, so he's completely bare. I take in his length, and swell inside. The second I touch my palm to him, it's like I've found my happy place again. His skin is so familiar as I stroke it, just like I used to. He's already stiff as a board but the second my hand moves faster, he gets even harder. Watching his head tip back from pleasure almost rips me to pieces; not able to take much longer, I let go and pull my panties off so we're completely bare on top of one another.

I don't even have time to argue about whether this is what I want. I know if I give in and listen to the pesky devil on my shoulder, she'll tell me to stop before I give myself fully to him again, but I shut her up the second I pull Rowen's body on top of my mine.

"Are you sure about this?" he asks, and I nod my head quickly.

"Are you still on the pill?" he whispers and I nod my head again, unable to speak. He mummers a "Thank God" and starts to inch himself into me.

When we were younger, it always took time, we had to go slow, my tiny body not ready for his, but now... no. Now, I'm slicker than a damn slipping slide on a mid-summer day. Once Rowen is in all the way, whispering sweet nothings in my ear the entire time, my body soaks him in. He gives me a slow thrust and then replaces it with a hard one, slamming into me over and over again. He's breathing deeply and mine mimics his. If it were possible for sparks to literally be flying from two people, they would be right now. They'd be coiled in between our bodies, sparking with each thrust like metal on metal. He rocks into me as one bare hand grips my leg and the other clutches my hair. His lips land on mine and our kiss is urgent and demanding.

"Sadie. Look at me," he demands in a strained voice. He pulls himself up on his hands and looks down at me, long eyelashes reaching almost up to his eyebrows. We stare at one another as he pulls out and jams into me again. Not able to take in his eyes, the way they're speaking to me in a completely different language, I let out a barely audible moan.

"I love you, Sadie." He groans, and I completely come undone. I come apart in every way possible; and he follows suit, landing on top of me, chest rising with each beat of his heart. The second the ecstasy wears off, I know I'm in trouble because he just took my entire heart, scars and all.

## TWENTY-FIVE

When Rowen rolls off me, we lay there for a long time, evening out our rushed breathing. I can tell he's looking at me, but I won't meet his gaze. Instead, I crawl over to him and lay my head on his bare chest, listening to his rapid heartbeat... probably for the last time.

He speaks, but it's in a deep whisper, brushing the loose strands of hair around my ear, "Remember last summer when I said there wasn't such a thing as bad luck or good luck? There's just luck?"

I nod my head against his chest, feeling his coiled hair scratch my chin. "Well, I think the entire last three years were good luck. Want to know why?" I nod my head again. "Because every single thing that happened in the last three years, led us straight to this moment. And let me tell you, that was a once in a lifetime moment we just had, Sadie."

I don't say anything; I just lean over and kiss the skin that lays over his heart. He tightens his hold on me and runs his fingers through my hair for the next hour. I pretend I'm asleep so he doesn't say anything else. Anything else that'll make me change my mind on what I'm going to do the very second he leaves.

Rowen slowly crawls out of my bed hours before the sun is set to rise. He carefully slips his jeans back on, careful not to make any noise. I lay perfectly still, not opening my eyes. Not even when he leans down to kiss my cheek and tell me he loves me, which only makes the hole in my stomach grow larger. I hear him slip out my window, and the second I hear it shut, the tears fall. They cascade down the sides of my face, soaking my pillow. I bury my face in my blankets, which are heavy with his scent, and that only makes me cry harder.

I may be rash in my decision to pack all my bags and head back to college two weeks early, but I have to. I have two choices: I can stay with Rowen, finish out the summer, and go back to college, hoping things stay the same. Hoping he doesn't leave me again, because that would no doubt destroy me. Or, I can go back to school tomorrow morning and run. It's no secret that I've fallen madly in love with him... deeper than ever but if I give him the chance to leave me, again... it will literally kill me. So, I'll do the killing for him. It'll be safer this way. I'll take my heart back and I'll stomp on it myself. I won't let him to do the stomping, because it won't be stomping. It'll be epically smooshing—leaving me with absolutely nothing but a wilted, trampled on, dying heart.

When Rowen and I were younger, our love was simple. It was puppy-love. That doesn't make it any less of a love that we have now, but it wasn't this... sacred. Our love back then wasn't this raw and life-changing. We were young; we had a love-at-first-sight type of love. Now, we have the Romeo and Juliet type of love... the kind that will kill you in the end.

When I text Rowen at six a.m. to meet me in front of the high school, before his practice starts, he sends me an "okay," followed by a question mark. I throw on my jean shorts, an old

ACDC shirt, and my white tennis shoes. I grab the three bags I packed, write my parents a tiny yet remorseful note saying I'd explain later, and drag myself to my little Ford to set out for the high school.

For the entire drive, the little devil and angel on my shoulder argue back and forth. The devil, pleased that I'm breaking my own heart instead of allowing Rowen to do it, again... and the angel, who is crying her pure, crystal blue tears, telling me I'm making the biggest mistake of my life. But the sight of Rowen, standing in his black workout pants and a loose t-shirt, shuts them both up. I have a frog in my throat that I keep pushing down further and further.

When I step out of the car, he rounds the front and takes in my face. He can tell I've been crying, no doubt.

"Sadie, what's wrong?" he asks, concerned. I take a deep breath and look out at the horizon, the sun barely peeking over the hills. It's a strange sight. There's the beautiful, bright sun about to unleash her yellow hue on the world, and then right above that, is the sharp contrast of the dark, deep night sky.

I choke, "I can't do this." And if Rowen's expression is portraying that he's surprised, I wouldn't know, because I can't look. I want to look. I want to memorize every tiny feature he has, just so my heart can hold onto something.

"What do you mean?" he questions, confused.

"I mean, I can't do this. Us."

It takes a few moments before he speaks again. "Why?" I cringe at his strained voice.

"I just can't, Rowen. I can't move past what happened three years ago. I can't move on. It's just... " I pause and swallow the frog again. "It's just better this way." My voice is no longer a normal tone, it's barely a whisper and I'm afraid he can tell just how much this is killing me. *It's better this way, Sadie*, I tell myself.

"Was this your grand plan? To make me fall in love with you all over again and then what? Leave me like I left you?" A jab strikes my heart.

"If I wanted to do that, I'd just leave without telling you goodbye." I meet his face and it's etched with pain. Good, maybe he'll just hate me and make this easier.

"That's bullshit. This is bullshit! You know that we belong together... " He is mad. Hurt and mad. He clenches his jaw so tightly I can see the muscles ticking.

"Rowen, this is what I want."

"No!" he yells, running his hands through his hair frantically. "Goddamnit, you know this isn't right. You and I, we belong together. Despite the past."

I say nothing, because I have no idea what to say. For a second, I rethink my decision. Maybe I should just take a chance, maybe things won't end up like before. Maybe he'll stay with me forever, but...

Maybe he won't. Suddenly all those memories and feelings I've been ignoring all summer come crashing into my mind like a thousand bats escaping a cave. The hurt, the loneliness, the heartbreak.

"Last summer, you said that I held the chess pieces. Well, this is what I'm doing with them. We don't belong together." I say, stronger than before, standing perfectly tall.

"NO! I'm taking them back. This isn't what you're doing with them!" he yells again, and I almost flinch.

"You can't just take them back, Rowen. This is what I want. Move on, be with someone who can fully be with you without having this ugly, wicked past always looming over them."

"I don't want anyone else, Sadie." I can literally hear my

heart ripping in half. I have to leave now, or else I won't. The pain in his voice ricochets throughout my body and I honestly want to plug my ears. *This is better, you're saving yourself. Go!*

I turn to leave, but his hand on my arms pulls me back. I shut my eyes quickly and turn around to face him again.

He whispers, tilting my head up with his hand. My eyes meet his and I know he can see right through me. "Is this really what you want? Will this make you happy? Being without me?"

I look at his eyes, his lips, his strong nose, his broad jawline—memorizing every single detail, then I muster up, "Yes." And his fingers leave my arm. He backs up, never leaving my gaze. I take the opportunity to jump in my car, and I mouth "I'm sorry" to him before taking off down the road, faster than ever.

I get the courage to peek in my rearview mirror and see him, standing there, looking completely defeated. His one arm is hanging loosely by his side and his other is at the bridge of his nose. The sun is casting a perfect glow behind him, almost outlining his body. I have to turn my gaze away, before I turn my car back around. Before I even make it out of the parking lot, a loud sob escapes my throat. It's a deep sob, uncontrollable, but I keep driving. I drive all the way until I get to that familiar, calming house out in the middle of nowhere. Where the farmland comforts me, as does the giant who tends to it.

I walk up to James' rickety wooden porch, and take a seat on his wooden, white rocking chair. He comes out of his house, slowly, taking one look at my face and then pulling out his handkerchief to hand to me. I use it to wipe the tears that won't stop. He sits beside me in the other chair, looking out at the distance. Giving me the silence that I need, for a little while.

"I think I gave you some bad advice." I turn my head and

take in his appearance. He's still wearing his jean overalls, stained with mud and dirt. I'm not sure how that's possible since it's barely reached seven in the morning.

He continues on, when I won't speak. "I told you to forgive but never forget, and I still stand by that. My mama was a smart woman, a brilliant woman. But, I learned something along this crazy ride of a life, Sadie."

I croak, "What's that?"

"When I said to forgive but never forget, I didn't mean for the never forgetting part to ruin your present. Never forgetting don't mean you need to be held back from what your heart wants; it just means you gotta to be stronger. Willing to fight so that thing you're never forgetting, don't happen again."

"But what if I can't help it from happening again?"

"There's ways around it, my sweet Sadie. There's always a detour, you just really have to look for it."

I let that sink in as we sit in silence for the next hour, peaceful in each other's presence. There's always a detour. So far, I haven't found one and I don't plan on it. Rowen and I, we're done. We're done so I can save myself from an even worse heartbreak.

# PART FOUR
# TWO MONTHS LATER

## SADIE & ROWEN

# TWENTY-SIX

ROWEN

When Sadie left two months ago, it nearly killed me. It ripped me in half. I'm not one to get too sappy and say how much it broke my heart into a million little pieces or anything, but it did. She fucking *destroyed* me. When she left, she took me with her. Not physically, that is, but in every other way possible.

She's always had me, even when she thought she didn't. After the attack three years ago, when I saw her lying in that hospital bed, tubes flowing from beneath her nose, gauze on her face, brown hair spread out all around her—even then she was the most beautiful thing I had ever seen.

I almost threw up that night, right there in her hospital room. Her mom was there, sleeping beside her on a small couch beneath the window. I walked over to the end of Sadie's bed and I couldn't hold back the silent tears. They fell from my face and landed on the end of her bed, where her feet were, underneath the white cotton blanket. I took one last look at her, feeling the pit in my stomach grow larger and then I left.

I left because I was ashamed, and confused. Then everything else just spiraled out of control. I left her lying there in that hospital bed and I'll probably never forgive myself for making that colossal mistake. But somehow Sadie learned to forgive me. It was like all my prayers had been answered from up above. I did everything I could to make it up to her, to show her that I love her and that I'd never leave her again.

But it wasn't enough.

She still left me in the end and here I am, sitting in my apartment on our shitty, cracked leather couch with Kyle going on about the latest football game he watched and I can't even focus on what he's truly saying. His voice is like background static, there enough that I can hear it, but I can't quite focus on it. I'm too busy thinking about Sadie and if I should have gone after her or not.

I've driven halfway to Duke and back, more times than I care to admit. It's embarrassing, really, how torn up I am about this entire situation. How I've almost driven over to her apartment to beg, literally beg on my hands and knees, for her to rethink this. For her to remember that she loves me just as much as I love her. But every time I saw a sign for Duke University, I'd turn my truck around, realizing that if there's one thing I know about Sadie, it's that she needs *time*.

Fucking time.

It's an annoying thing if you think about it. Always waiting. The clock is always ticking and time is *always* running out.

I just hope it doesn't run out before she comes back to me.

Because in the end, we belong together. Even if there's one more second left in this world, *we belong together*.

I can promise you that.

SADIE

It only took me two months to realize that I made a gigantic mind-blowing mistake. Two whole months. Denial took up most of those two months. Isn't that a thing? Five stages of grief; denial, anger, bargaining, depression, and acceptance? I unquestionably denied the fact that I ripped my own heart out and fed it to the wolves. I pretended that Rowen and I never happened. It got to the point that even Alicia was concerned. I brushed off any conversation she wanted to have about him. I avoided talking about him at all costs with Hannah Marie and Anna *and* even my parents. My dad was thrilled, of course. He didn't want to talk about Rowen, ever again. And I was right there with him.

After having a long conversation with my mom about facing "whatever it was that happened between Rowen and I," I landed smack dab in the anger stage. I was pissed. I was so freaking pissed off at myself that I wanted to bang my head off the wall repeatedly until I forgot his name. How could I have been so damn stupid to let myself fall for him, *again*? After everything? After everything we had been through I should have known that it wouldn't end up good. Rowen and I are like this giant ticking time bomb, ready to explode at the first little hiccup, and did we ever. Explode, that is. I haven't talked to him at all. I ignored every single call he made for the next few weeks after I left for college. He even went so far as to call Alicia, who also ignored him, per my request.

Then came the bargaining. *"I'll only look on his social media to make sure he's okay, that he's happy."* But, Alicia wouldn't let me and I didn't want to start my own social media just to stalk my ex-ex-boyfriend. That was a little ridiculous and borderline close to being that same seventeen year old who nursed a broken heart years ago.

So, after the bargaining had passed, the depression and acceptance came in waves. I cried and cried and cried for the stupid decision(s) I'd made; not only getting involved with Rowen again, but falling in love, and then running away like a little schoolgirl who was offered candy from the creep in the white van. I played the words that James spewed to me over and over again during my binge ice cream devouring marathons for weeks on end. *A detour*. I had no idea what that crazy old man was talking about until one day, it just *clicked*. I was in my senior thesis class, absentmindedly scrawling notes and BOOM, it connected. It hit me harder than a head-on collision crash.

I didn't want to forget about the last four years of my life; some of my best memories were in those four years. My first kiss with Rowen, my first real laugh after the attack, the second time I fell in love with him. I didn't want to forget, I *couldn't* forget about those things, just like I couldn't forget about him leaving me and breaking my heart. I would pray that all the bad would go away. That I could be normal again. That I could fall in love and not have this undeniable feeling creeping up my back but it never went away.

Then it just clicked; I didn't want to forget all of the painful memories between Rowen and I because that's what formed this new passionate, bottomless love for him. The way I love him so fiercely is *because* of the pain. I needed to embrace it, I needed to remember that I did pick myself back up after the attack, I picked myself up after my best friend betrayed me, and I picked myself up when Rowen left me. *I* picked myself up. The detour was *embracing it*. I had to embrace it all, not hide it under a ratty old kitchen rug. I wouldn't be able to stop Rowen or anyone from breaking my heart but I could learn to make myself happy again. I could learn how to make myself feel *full* again. I understood. I understood the detour; I just needed to get around all the damn roadblocks in my way. I *finally* understood the wisest words I have ever heard, and they all came from a sweet old man who leads such a simple life.

And that's why I'm about to go find Rowen, right now. I sprang out of my chair, leaving my notes on my desk, and high-tailed it to my car. UNC isn't that far from Duke, and besides, even if he was on the other side of the country right now soaking up California rays, I'd still drive my tiny Ford all the way over there.

This was something I had to do in person. I needed to grab him by the face and pour my deranged heart out to him. I was so stupid to let our love go because I was scared, because I was scared of the past. It's never going to go away; and it's time to face those steep hills. You only get one life, right?

The moment I shut my car door and turn the key in the ignition, I get the eerie feeling that someone is watching me. Campus isn't extremely busy at the moment; there are only a few students lollygagging around during the early afternoon, but there's one person in the distance, staring directly at me.

Her bright pink dress stands out against the blue sky and green grass; she looks like a movie star with her bright blonde hair cut close to her head. It's styled in a way that only models can pull off, or Hallie Berry.

I stare at her for little longer and twist my head to the side. That's when my eyes almost fall out of my head. *"Holy shit,"* I whisper, as the girl starts walking towards my car with her right arm up, waving.

*Samantha.*

What is she doing here?

My fingers skim over the automatic button on my door panel and soon my passenger side window is rolling down.

When Samantha appears in front of it, I scan her face. She looks different. Skinnier, but healthy. Her high cheek-bones are shining brightly with a pink hue, and then she smiles and it's... genuine.

"Hi, Sadie," she says, smiling even bigger.

"What—what... " At a complete loss for words, I shake my head and start again. "What are you doing here?"

"Well, I came here to see you." Samantha bends down and crosses her arms on the ledge of my window. If she had an ulterior plan to be the world's biggest bitch, like usual, I could just push the window button and bye-bye she'd go. But something seems different, so I'm giving her the benefit of the doubt.

When I don't muster up a response, she continues. "I was on my way to your apartment and then sure enough, I saw you getting into your car. In a hurry, might I add," she chuckles. "I came here... " She looks around for a brief second, then gestures to my door. "Do you mind?"

I feel leery but regardless, I let her in.

Once the door slams shut, and she adjusts her pink dress over her bony knees, she looks out the windshield, staring at the few students wandering about with book bags slung over their backs.

"I came here to say... I'm sorry."

Silence fills the car. It's a noticeable silence, too. Filled with awkward tension. I don't know what to say. I used to daydream about the day that Samantha would say sorry to me, what it would feel like to have such a long-lost friend, apologize for being... crazy. I used to think it wouldn't matter but sitting here with her... it does.

"I wish I could say that I had this epic moment in my life that made me realize how bad of a person I was and how I wanted to apologize for being a bad friend to you. But it didn't quite pan out like that... " My eyebrows crinkle, waiting for her next words. "Sadie... "

I turn my body towards her, taking in her face. Then I feel as if I've been slapped across the face. I was *not* expecting the next words out of her mouth. The words, "I had cancer." I let out a gasp and leave my mouth hanging wide open.

"Samantha," I breathe. "Are... are you okay?" *Nice, Sadie. What a stupid question to ask.*

"Oh! Yes, I'm okay now. Sorry! I should have started off with that," she titters. "They removed the tumors and the chemo worked. I'm better. Healthy."

I reach over and grab her lone hand that's lying palm down on her thigh. I give it a long squeeze, suddenly realizing why her hair is cut so short and why she seems so *different*.

"I'm so glad you're okay now. I'm truly sorry you had to endure that," I say, genuinely. But a small part of me wonders whether she's lying. She's lied in the past, several times. But just seeing her tiny body sitting here in my car, hair cut short, cheekbones sticking out, I can tell that something major has happened to her. Not just on the outside, either. On the inside, she seems like a different person.

As she squeezes my hand back, she takes a deep breath. "It was awful. The entire thing. I was so sick. I threw up so many times. And let me tell you something," she turns to me and grins, "Throwing up from chemotherapy is a lot worse than throwing up because you drank too much."

We laugh together for a few seconds, breaking up the awful tension in the air. "But it's sad that it took a near life-ending moment to realize that I was a *terrible* person. All the bad things I'd done in the past caught up to me pretty quick."

I watch as she bites her lip and ponders for a moment. "I promised myself that if I got better, that if I made it out alive, I'd try to undo all the bad things I did. Starting with you."

I didn't say anything in response because I just didn't know what would be appropriate in this moment. Her actions can't ever truly be justified but that doesn't mean I can't accept her apology. Right? I mean I should know better than anyone that sometimes forgiving someone is okay.

My voice barely over a whisper, "It's okay, Samantha. I forgive you."

"It's not okay. Look what I did." Her face contorts to the point that I think she's going to cry. "I ruined you and Rowen. When I heard you two had gotten back together, though, it honestly made some of that guilt from what I'd done go away."

I start to tell her that Rowen and I aren't technically together anymore but she stops me with her hand. "I also know that you're not together anymore... and I know that's my fault, too."

Interjecting, I say, "It's not your fault. It's mine." Then I inhale, letting my shoulders fall. "I messed up, Samantha."

We both stare out the windshield for a little while, not talking. It's peaceful to be this close to her without feeling like I want to yell at her, or smack her. A part of me feels healed, like I've needed this all along.

After a few minutes pass, Samantha peeks over at me. "Sadie, take it from me. Life is too short. Don't waste it."

I bite my lip and nod. She smiles at me, the creases in her eyes deepening, and I know she can probably read my mind, just like we used to do years ago.

"I'm going after him." I say, with confidence blooming from within.

"Good. Go get your man, Sadie." We both laugh, and she exits the car but not before leaning down to squeeze my hand again.

Her eyes holding hope, "Call me, okay?"

"I will."

Then I back out of my spot and head to UNC for Rowen.

I'll fix this. I'll make it right.

# TWENTY-SEVEN

ROWEN

Walking through my life in a murky haze is normal for me now. Not caring about much, unless it has to do with a brown-haired girl named Sadie, and yep. That's about it. I hate feeling like this. So... pent up. Just waiting. Wondering. Imagining. I fucking hate it and I hate that Kyle can see right through my bullshit.

That's why I'm laughing along with him and our other friends right now, about to go get some lunch. I need to get him off my back because knowing Kyle, he'll call me out on my shitty mood and then it'll make me even more pissed. So, faking it is my best bet right now.

"They called us... and I quote... 'scissor sisters'!" Our friend Sarah is fuming, arms crossed over her chest, face red and eyes wide. "I'm pissed!"

Kyle cracks up so hard and I start to snicker beside him which earns me a smack from the back of Sarah's hand.

"Stop! This is not okay. I think that in this society, being gay should be completely acceptable. Don't you?" She looks at me and I nod my head quickly. Of course it should be accepted. Who cares?

"Relax, Sarah. They're probably just jealous that you're not interested in them." I say.

"Damn straight they are! I'm hot."

I chuckle again, throwing my arm around her shoulders to loosen up her tense posture. "I'm sorry, but I just have to say it... "scissor sisters" is a hilarious name."

Sarah turns her head towards me, her red hair skimming my arm, and breaks into a huge grin. I let out a forced laugh before Kyle grabs my attention.

"Uh, Rowen?" Kyle says from a few feet away from me. I look over at him, waiting for him to say something snarky about my attitude, but his mouth is wide open, staring across the student lot.

When my eyes find her, I stop dead in my tracks. I take a gulp of air as I see Sadie's tiny tanned frame basically dive into her driver's seat.

My heart beats like a fucking boombox in my chest as I drop my arm from Sarah's shoulders, ignoring her question about what's going on and take off like my life depends on it. My legs are striding further apart than they ever have, but I keep pushing to get to her. I almost can't believe my eyes. I almost can't believe she's here. She's here at UNC.

Just as I reach the curb, I stop. Sadie's in her car and yelling her name seems to only make her go faster. Before I know it, she's backing up quickly, almost mowing down a student and then speeding off into the distance. I reach my hands up and place them on my head. *No. This isn't happening. Go after her. Make her believe you fucking love her!* I take off in the opposite direction, reaching into my jingling pocket and fetch my keys. I jump in my truck so fast I don't even get the door shut. I drive with one hand and dial her number with the other. My fingers trembling along the touchscreen and when she ignores my call for the third time, I press my foot as hard as it'll go on the accelerator. She's not getting away this time; she came here for a reason and I'm going to be that reason. I have to be that reason. I just fucking have to.

SADIE

The second I park my car in the student lot, I whip the sunvisor down to make sure I don't look as nervous as I feel. I wipe the tear-smudged mascara away from my eyes, run my fingers through my long hair, and lick my lips, giving myself one last nod.

When I step out of the car, I realize that I have no freaking idea where he is in this moment. But, I would search every single classroom, every single dorm room.

Every.

Square.

Inch.

Of this campus until I found him, ripped my heart out and handed it to him, blood dripping and all. I needed to do this. I needed him. *I need Rowen.*

I'm not sure if it was fate laughing at me, or if the world really is this freaking wicked, but it was like there were a thousand neon lights with arrows pointing down at his chestnut brown hair, walking casually across the sidewalk with a group of friends. My heart consticts in my chest as I take one step towards him before my heart stops beating altogether.

There is Rowen. There is *my* Rowen, standing there with his arm wrapped around a tall redhead's shoulders. He is wearing a maroon t-shirt, throwing his head back, laughing. I bet if I listen hard enough, I can hear that melodic voice through the crowded murmurs of students walking to and from classes but I don't. Instead, I gasp out loud, using my one hand to cover my mouth while the other clenches at my churning stomach.

*I'm too late. I'm. Too. Late.* He's moved on. He's... happy. I almost can't take it, I almost can't stand here watching his life unfold, but I do. I stand here and watch because if there's one thing that will keep me alive in this moment, it's the fact that he's happy.

I take one step backward, then another, and another, my eyes never wavering, until I'm right at my car door. I watch him cross the emerald green grass to get to the parking lot, taking my soul with him. I can tell it was Kyle walking beside him, holding a petite blonde's hand, and then his eyes land on me. Kyle's boyish face has never looked so confused and at alert until then.

I knew I was caught. My eyes widen and I duck into the driver's seat of my car, welcoming my Hawaiian air freshener. My window is down so I hear Kyle yell my name, but I ignore it because if Kyle saw me, then Rowen did, too. Now, I'm just stuck. Do I stay and make up an excuse? I can't ruin his happiness now. It means so much more to me than my own; I close my eyes at the thought and give my head a sharp shake. That's how you know you truly love someone, ya know? Putting their happiness before your own, even if you feel like you are literally dying right there, in that very second.

"Sadie!" Rowen's voice cuts straight through me and the tears come right after the slice.

"Sadie! Wait!" *Slice. Slice. Slice.* He is frantic and out of breath but that doesn't stop me from turning my key and backing the hell out of there. I back out so fast that I almost hit another college student. I hear them yell and just as I look back to make sure they are still alive, I see Rowen running full speed at my car, hair blown back and everything.

*Keep going, don't let him see how much this is killing you. He's happy. He's happy, just go.*

So that's what I did. I went.

My phone is already vibrating frantically in my cup holder and I know it's Rowen, but I ignore it. I ignore it as I head straight for the highway. I am damn close to the freeway when my phone starts up again. He is going to make this hard. *Why is everything just so hard?*

I shove my foot down on the accelerator, as if making my car move faster is going to make Rowen stop calling me. Like it's going to make everything better. I should have known that running away from my problems wouldn't work—it never has before; I should have known the second I heard the squealing tires that I messed up... in more ways than one. I should have known. *I should have freaking known.*

The angry pain right after the loudest noise that I have ever heard, except for that eerie gun-shot I heard years ago, hits me like a ton of crumbling bricks. I knew something was wrong when I heard the outside shouts, glass crunching, and loud screaming coming from my own mouth. I look down in front of me and the only thing I see is something that resembls a big white fully down pillow, so I do what anyone else would have done; I let my head hang low enough to rest against it and I pretend that everything is fine. Even though, it isn't.

ROWEN

I think I've died. Everything feels so out of reach to me, yet I can touch everything in sight. The muscle that thumps in my chest hurts with every single beat. The last three hours have moved so fast but so slow at the same time.

When I finally caught up to Sadie's car, I saw it on the side of the highway. The front was smashed in, the silver color that always shined so bright in the sun was tarnished, and the windshield was cracked. I pulled over so quickly that my tires squealed in response. I ran over to her car and saw her limp body being pulled out, and I almost passed out. I swear to God I saw black spots in my vision. But then things moved even faster and I had no time to faint. I fought the EMT workers so hard that I almost smashed one of their faces in. They finally let me in the ambulance with her.

She was awake for a little while, confused. Disoriented. Agitated. Her little body thrashing on the gurney, her brown locks whipping in front of her face. I grabbed her hand, trying to coax her to calm down but she ripped it out of mine tried to get up, screaming when she moved her right leg. That's when the burly EMT worker finally gave her a shot to calm her down.

And that's when I begged for them to give it to me, too. I felt myself breaking from the inside out. I sat, unmoving, trying to calm my erratic breathing down, and the only time it slowed was a couple hours later, when I caught wind that she'd be fine.

I called her parents right when we got to the hospital, my voice shaking with fear for Sadie. It took them a little while to get here because Sadie drove all the way to UNC. I figured her dad would kill me on sight, for once again being in a hospital with his daughter who was hurt and I was fine. But, surprisingly he didn't. Once they realized that Sadie was okay, her mom hugged me tight, allowing my eyes to drip with tears. Then her dad grabbed my shoulder and squeezed it, hard. He tipped his head down and I knew, even without saying the words, that he wasn't angry with me. Maybe he could see the pain on my face. Maybe he could see that I was a complete fucking mess.

I had told him, almost three months ago, that I loved Sadie

and that I would never, ever stop loving her. That I would take care of her. I would make her happy, and this is me keeping my promise. I'm here. I'm here now, and I'm ready to take care of her. I'm done waiting. I don't care if she wakes up after her surgery and never wants to see me again.

I'm not leaving.

And I'm not letting her run.

I would rather cut my own heart out than let her run from me again.

So, I'll sit here in this pale blue waiting area outside her hospital room until the second she wakes up and tell her just that.

# TWENTY-EIGHT

SADIE

Peeling my eyes open from underneath my eyelids was a terrible idea. The bight, fluorescent lights goaded the throbbing in my left temple to a pain so extreme that I couldn't even put it into words. I squeeze my eyes shut again, trying to recall where I was and why my head hurt so bad. The lights above took me to different time, and a different place. *The hospital,* five years ago after I was beaten half to death on the floor of that damn chicken place.

*No.*

*No.*

*No. I am not at the hospital again.* I am not reliving a nightmare. NO. Life can't simply be that cruel to me, right? The first time I landed in the hospital years ago was a disastrous, fluke, a once-in-a-lifetime thing. I couldn't possibly have two FREAK incidents happen in my life to land me in the hospital like this again.

*Oh my God! My face!* I instantaneously reach up and touch all around my face, keeping my eyes shut. My fingers touch the barely-there ridges of my old scar, stopping for a brief second, and then resuming to touch the rest of my face. I slowly rub my shaking fingers over the ridge of my tiny nose, up to my forehead—feeling the minuscule hair of my eyebrows, back down to my jaw. Nothing new. There aren't any other scarring ridges anywhere. My face is fine. I'm fine. I think.

I slowly creep my eyes open, eyelashes fluttering against each other before allowing my eyes to welcome the light. I try to recall what happened to land me in the hospital, but the only thing I can hear inside my head is Rowen's name. Then comes the rest. Rowen. Redhead. Kyle. Chasing. Driving... . *crash*. I got in a crash. The flashes of images come back to me one after another. Pounding in my skull, heartbeat picking up with each recollection.

This is happening again. I'm in the hospital, with who knows how many injuries (at least my face is okay, right?) and the only thing I can think to want is Rowen. And he's not going to be here. He's not going to be here again because I messed everything up. He's not going to be here to comfort me like I need. It's like I'm having déjà vu, except the pain isn't on my face, it's near my lower extremities.

When my eyes open fully, breath still coming out in huge huffs, panic about to swallow me up whole—I see my mom's big brown eyes peering down at me. Her soft palm slides down my face the second I feel her warm breath on my cheek.

"Hi, sweetie," she whispers and I instantly want to crawl in her lap like I'm three years old again.

"Mom." My voice comes out raspy like I've been in the desert for years. I let out a little cough and I didn't even have to ask her for a drink. Before I know it, the straw is in between my lips and the cool water splashes around my mouth, coating the back of my throat.

"Thanks," I say, sitting up a little in my bed.

"The doctor said you'd be up soon, and I didn't believe him," my dad says, from the bottom of my bed. My eyes widen at the stark white cast my leg is in. My mouth gapes, and I suck in a breath.

"My leg... "

"Oh, honey, it's fine. You broke it and they had to re-set it, that's why you've been out so long." I look over at my mom once more, noticing the bags under her eyes. "That's the only injury you sustained, besides a mild concussion." I don't say anything for so long that it becomes awkward.

"Do you remember what happened?" she asks, and I want to say no. I want to say no and pretend I didn't drive to UNC to profess my love to Rowen and then drive like a maniac to get away from him and end up wrecking. I didn't want to admit it, but I did anyway.

"Yes." It comes out as a whisper, my ashamed feelings pouring out of me in the form of one single word.

See, the thing is... Rowen and I... it always ends in one of us wrecking the other. No pun intended. We always go around this never-ending circle of hurting one another—no, not a circle, more like an infinity symbol like we're chasing one another around the loops that never seem to disappear. I can even hear the annoying Buzz Lightyear toy in my head yelling, "To infinity and beyond," repetitively as if he's a broken record. Is this how it's always going to be? Having such an unbearable amount of pain just for a little bit of love and happiness with him? Is it even worth it?

The answer is, yes. *Yes, it is.*

"What exactly happened, babe?" my dad says, keeping his face nice and steady. Calm.

I bite the inside of my mouth, trying to come up with a better excuse. Trying to come up with anything that doesn't make me sound pathetic and as lovesick as I really am, but nothing measures up. So, I spill. I put it all out in the open.

"He, he was happy and I tried to get away so he wouldn't see me. I didn't want to make things worse." I hiccup, holding my sob in. I rambled so fast that I'm not even sure they caught I word I said.

Before they could say anything, I cry out, "It's fine. I'll be fine this time. Don't worry. I can pick myself back up, after the cast is off... " I give a tiny but painful side-smile and my parents say nothing. They look over at one another, and I see my mom grin. My eyebrows fold into themselves and I cock my head. *What the hell?*

Before I could ask anything else, my dad turns and walks out of the room. My mouth is ajar but I quickly closed it, trying to make sense of what just happened. Surely, he can't be mad at me. I just got in a wreck for goodness sake; that should give me *some* pity points.

Watching my mom depart from the room right after my dad, I was about to yell out when I heard a loud bang coming from the hallway, like someone had fallen over a cart of medical supplies. Then... all the air in the room was swallowed up by my large intake of breath.

Surprised.

Confused.

Overwhelmed.

And then relief slapped me in the face.

"Rowen," I whisper,

"You're awake," he says, red-faced. He is definitely out of breath, striding over to the side of my hospital bed. His maroon shirt is wrinkled around his waist and his dark hair is standing in about twelve different directions. He looks completely shaken up.

The second he gets to the side of my bed, I sit up a little

straighter. I stare at his glossed-over brown eyes and feel the need to pinch myself to see if I am dreaming. It doesn't feel real. It doesn't feel real to be sitting in this bed, with a broken leg, after running away from a boy I love with my entire heart, only for him to be standing beside me now looking completely disheveled.

"What are you doing here?" I ask, never taking my eyes off his. I watch him blink three times before he backs away and drags a chair over right next to me, plopping down in it and leaning his head against my arm.

His breath is warm and choppy when he begins to speak, "Sadie, I promised myself a long time ago that I would *always* be here for you. That I would never, ever not be here for you again. I fucked up so bad the last time you were in the hospital. I will never put you through that again. Ever." His voice is hoarse and strained, like saying these words are literally painful.

"But—" I start. "But, you and the girl, and... " He cuts me off before I can say anything else.

When his head jerks up to meet mine, all I see is tender love. "Sadie, that girl you saw me with... is my friend, Sarah. My friend, Sarah, who is dating our other friend, Abigail."

My mouth forms an "O," just as Rowen's forms a small, playful grin—a small, playful grin that makes my heart skip a beat.

Despite the pain in my leg, I feel... light. I feel like I'm invincible. Maybe I am dead. *Am I in heaven?* The rational part of my brain knows I'm not because I'm pretty damn sure there isn't any pain in heaven, physical or not, and there is definitely an extreme pain coming from my right leg.

"Sadie. How could you ever think that I could move on from you? Haven't you been paying any attention to the last few years? I would do anything for you. I would do anything to make you happy."

I gulpbefore he grabs my hand and squeezes it tightly. "The only reason I didn't go after you was because I knew I had to rethink my plan. I knew exactly what I needed to do after I sat down and let the shock wear off. You needed *time*.

"You've always needed time, Sadie. I mean, it took you an *entire* year to think about being friends with me again. Then it took you another year to realize that you were still in love with me. Why would this be any different? I knew you would come back to me again; I just had to give you some time to figure it out in that pretty little head of yours."

I knew I was blushing on the outside while basically exploding on the inside. He knows me so well. He knows me better than I know myself.

I clench my teeth so hard to keep the tears from streaming down my cheeks. I grab his hand, pulling him onto my bed with me and he willingly came, weighing down the bed so much that I think it might collapse.

When he turns his head toward mine, our faces only inches apart, he looks me right in the eye and says, "I love you Sadie, and I'm not afraid to say it."

Moving my face even closer to his, lips brushing over his as I spoke, "I'm not afraid either... not anymore."

His eyes light up, and he presses his lips to mine, cupping my face in his hands. The second our lips reconnect, I know that with Rowen is *exactly* where I need to be.

"I'm never letting you go again," he whispers against my lips.

I whisper right back, "Me either."

The End

## ACKNOWLEDGMENTS

I first want to thank my family for their endless amount of support. They will probably always be at the top of my list for acknowledgments because I couldn't do this without them! Especially Joe, my husband! Thanks for being the best husband in the world, I love you!

I also want to thank my friend Stephanie at editS, for editing my work and for being so amazing at catching those annoying grammatical errors (especially all the unnecessary commas that I like to throw in random sentences... LOL). You helped me make this book come to life so thank you, dear friend!

To my new online friend, Megan, thank you answering all of my questions regarding formatting and KDP. I was in tears and you saved me, so thank you times a million!

Lastly, I want to thank every single person who read my book and took a chance on a new author! Putting my work out there is scary but to have such support from you readers is amazing! You rock!!

Xo!

## ABOUT S.J. SYLVIS

S.J. Sylvis is a lover of reading and writing and just recently graduated with her graduate degree focusing on English and Creative Writing (the only fun parts where the writing classes). Besides writing, S.J. Sylvis loves coffee (specifically caramel iced coffee, but really, any coffee will do), binge-watching Gilmore Girls, going to the beach and spending time with her family! She currently lives in Louisiana but is often moving as her husband is in the United States Marine Corps and they go where the military sends them!

Please be on the look out for S.J. Sylvis's next release, JUST MAYBE, coming out Summer, 2018!

Find S.J. Sylvis online:
www.sjsylvis.wordpress.com

facebook.com/sjsylvisbooks

twitter.com/authorsjsylvis

instagram.com/authorsjsylvis

11721290R00129

Made in the USA
Lexington, KY
14 October 2018